TIMBER

The Mountain Man's Babies

FRANKIE LOVE

Frankie Love

COPYRIGHT

Edited by Larks&Katydids

Cover by Mayhem Cover Creations

ABOUT THE BOOK

TIMBER

Jax

I've been called wild. Dirty. Untamed.
I moved to the woods to get away from the bullsh*t of the city. People there don't understand a man like me.
I work hard, and my hands are as calloused as my heart.
And nothing's gonna change that.
But now I've met Harper.
And my whole f*cking world has changed.
But this girl keeps running.
I need to make her stay because she's having my baby.

Harper

I never expected my fiancé to break things off. I'd saved myself for my wedding night, and now I'm left wondering why.

Needing to get away, I ran to my uncle's cabin in the woods.

But a storm has left me stranded on Jax's doorstep, and soon enough he takes me in his arms.

And on the floor. And on the table. And in the great outdoors.

Our time together has left me with a big problem ... a problem a wild man like him can't fix.

A problem that makes me run ... because I need a man who believes in true love and commitment.

I need a man who is ready to be a father.

WARNING: This story contains graphic language and an untamed man who takes a virgin. Please don't read if you're not ready for hot sex that will make you reach for that vibrator hidden under your pillow. If the batteries are out, your own hand will do.

No shame, babycakes. Enjoy this steamy story! You deserve it.

TIMBER
The Mountain Man's Babies
FRANKIE LOVE

CHAPTER ONE

JAX

I SWING down against the trunk a final time before getting out of the way. I call out to Buck, making sure he moves.

My dog, Jameson, barks wildly as he watches the swaying pine.

The tree falls with a strong, heavy rush that sends a chill over my skin.

It happens every time.

I feel most alive when I've taken something, using my own hands, and brought it to the ground.

I used to do that with women. There was nothing I liked more than fucking a woman I'd just met, giving them my solid wood, something they would remember. Then they could go home to their pansy-ass boyfriend or husband, and think of my trunk when someone else tried to get them off.

But then things changed. Fucking a woman I didn't know got me in trouble.

With everyone.

And I had to get the fuck out of town.

I moved out of the city a few months ago, and I haven't looked back. I came out here, to the dense forest.

The only thing I miss about life back in Coeur d'Alene is the women. While I find a lot of raccoons in these parts, good pussy isn't as common as it was back home.

Now, instead of taking a woman hard and fast, I swing my axe. Some guys might use a chainsaw, but I like the feel of the blade biting into the wood. The power in each stroke.

I take down pine trees. I call myself an old-school lumberjack, but that's mostly just a joke I tell myself. I'm not doing anything with this pile of wood besides burning some of it and putting the rest in a heap at the side of the cabin.

I watch as the tree falls; timber.

"That was a big-ass motherfucker," Buck says, taking a swig from the beer I gave him when he showed up an hour ago.

Buck owns the gas station and post office in town and drops off any packages I receive. I avoid town as much as possible.

"Damn straight," I agree, dropping the axe blade into the base of the chopped tree.

I pull off my leather gloves and then run my hand over my thick beard as I assess the fallen pine. It will take me most of the week to cut this tree into stackable pieces.

"You wanna come down the mountain, head to the bar?"

I don't want to laugh in Buck's face—but the last thing I wanna do is sit on some plastic stool in a podunk bar, drinking cheap beer and listening to Buck and his big game–hunting buddies talk shit.

I'd rather sit in my own goddamned chair. I'd rather drink my own goddamned beer. And I sure as hell would rather listen to silence than discuss target practice.

I may live in the sticks, but I'm no motherfucking hillbilly.

My mother calls me a modern day Thoreau. I don't really give a shit what that means—but I think it means I like to sit in the quiet and think.

I also like to swing my axe. As I've mentioned. It's the only sane thing in the world anymore. The only thing I can, without question, hold onto. Everything else is liable to fall apart.

"I don't like that scene. You know that, Buck. Not sure why you keep asking."

"I'm asking because you're the crazy fool living in the woods, talking to yourself. You don't even have wi-fi out here."

"That's intentional."

Buck doesn't understand why I don't go into town with him. It's mostly because I have no interest in discussing my personal shit with anyone—especially him.

"Yeah, well, it's January. This shit's gonna get cold real fast."

"It's cold already," I tell him as we cross back to my cabin, passing the frosted tips of the pine trees. Jameson trails us as we make our way over the icy earth, the ground crunching with each step.

"Well, you're the fool who moved out to the woods at the end of fall, not me," Buck says. "Just wanna make sure you don't become a recluse."

I don't tell Buck that being a recluse is exactly what I'm after.

"I'll see you around then. And stop by the store if you need anything, ya hear?" Buck heads to his big pickup truck, hollering as he swings open the door, "Oh, and thanks for the beer, Jax. Though I'm not sure what that shit was." He gives a hearty laugh as he turns the ignition.

Fucking fool, I think, shaking my head. He doesn't know what home-brewed beer is. I may be living in the woods, but I have a kegerator all hooked up inside my cabin. I brew beer, and it's the good stuff.

I watch him backing down the drive, grateful to see him go. He's a good guy, but I prefer my own company these days.

Heading to my cabin, I let Jameson in. I notice that snowflakes have begun to fall as the night sets in. I shut my door, knowing I need to add wood to my fire if I'm gonna stay warm tonight.

There sure as hell isn't anything out in these parts to get me heated up.

HARPER

The tires on my modest hatchback come to a dead halt, in the dead of winter, in what is quickly becoming the dead of night. I'm trying not to full-on panic.

I remind myself of the quote that's my new life motto—that is to say, the quote I read while

I scrolled through Pinterest this morning at a gas station on my way out of Boise. I was deleting every single wedding picture I'd pinned, and came across this classic gem:

Keep Calm and Carry On

Okay, so I know it's cheesy, but I've gotta hold onto something right now. If I don't, I'll fall apart.

And I can't fall apart until I've at least pulled up at my uncle's cabin.

Which should be right here. Or right ... somewhere.

This would all be a lot easier if 1) it hadn't grown pitch dark in, like, four seconds, 2) Google maps would pull up on my phone, and 3) it wasn't snowing.

And these flakes are coming down fast. This hatchback isn't four-wheel anything. It doesn't even have four seats.

How did I end up here? Oh, right, my fiancé ditched me a week before our wedding.

I drop my head against the steering wheel, not wanting to lose it, pinching my eyes closed tight. A full-on sob will not get me somewhere warm and toasty and safe.

I quickly lift my head as the horn on my car begins to blast. This is about the same time I realize that, if I want to be warm and toasty tonight, I'm going to have to light the fire myself.

In the dark.

This wasn't the greatest plan.

Keep Calm and Carry On.

I blink back my tears and scan the old logging road. I doubt anyone has been out here in ages. My own uncle said it's been two summers since he came.

But I have nowhere else to go. I want to avoid the social media meltdown that will surely ensue once everyone gets word about Luke ditching me.

My parent didn't want me to go alone, which under normal circumstance I would understand. I still live under the covering of my parents, and believe that they know what's best for me.

But this is different. We were all shocked by Luke's choice—after all, he and I had courted for two years. He had become family. So when I insisted that I needed some time away on my own, my family helped me find a place where I could ride out this storm. I spent twenty-one years earning their trust and they know I would never allow myself to get into a compromising position.

And my uncle offered his old cabin, which was so generous of him. I don't come from gobs of money. Or even slivers of cash. I come from humble people, I'm the daughter of a hard-working preacher.

It's not like we have lake houses and time shares—and even if we did, they wouldn't be wi-fi free.

Which was my one and only request when I told my family I needed some time away.

Granted, wi-fi would be really helpful at the moment, as I can't get my bearings and have no clue where my uncle's cabin actually is.

Besides, my car is stuck in this snow. I'm not going anywhere.

This is the time a normal girl would cry.

But I'm not a normal girl. I was raised to keep my chin up, to be grateful in all circumstances. To believe that everything happens for a reason. Even the worst things.

Even things like having a broken heart. Because even if my heart got broken in the process of Luke leaving me, it's better that it happened now instead of a month from now.

Still ... I'm going to need a lot of time to heal.

Biting my lip, I try to think through my next step. I'll freeze if I stay in this car tonight; even though it's stuffed to the gills with blankets and provisions, I know it can drop to freezing in the Idaho State Forest in January.

Heaven knows I don't want to die tonight.

I close my eyes, and ask for a sign.

When I open them, it's like a miracle. Through the windshield, in the distance, I see a tiny trail of smoke reaching the clear night sky.

Whoever lit that fire is my Savior. I need to find him.

CHAPTER TWO

JAX

SITTING by the fire in a leatherback rocker, I contemplate throwing on another log. But I'm wearing jeans and a buttoned flannel, and it's pretty toasty in here already.

Instead I unbutton my shirt and then pick up the rag I've been using to polish my axe blade.

Okay, I know I love this fucking thing, but I'm not some axe murderer. I just know tomorrow's work will go a lot easier if I have a sharp tool to hack at wood with.

I call it work, but I know it's not a job. I'm through with the bullshit of running a company in a city where assholes are in charge.

So now I polish an axe blade instead of

running the trucking company I built from the ground up. Well, that I built with my best friend, Dean.

Sleeping with the Sherriff's daughter got me into trouble–which really fucked with our business plan. Dean was pissed I slept with her because next thing we knew Sherriff Martin was doing anything in his power to screw with us ... namely me.

It wasn't my fault, I didn't know who the hell she was. The next thing I knew we had taxes and fees slapped on our fucking truckloads every time I went to the weigh station.

Sherriff Martin wanted me out of Coeur d'Alene. That's bullshit. No man can tell me what I can do. I left on my own terms.

I can sleep with who I want, when I want.

And the last thing I wanted was to screw over Dean. I'm not a motherfucking asshole. I took my name off the ledgers and became a silent partner.

And got the fuck out of there.

Now, my life has become pretty damn familiar. But I knew that would happen when I decided to ship out here, set up my man-cave in the woods.

Jameson starts barking like a goddamned fool, and I shake my head. I love my Irish wolfhound, but he gets all wiry out here in the woods, in a way he never was in the city. Every noise, every rustle, every gust of wind causes his ears to stand, his back to arch.

Maybe it's just that out here he feels alive. I can relate.

Jameson is going nuts now, barking up a real shitstorm.

"Goddamn it, what's your deal?" I ask, standing. I walk to the window and pull back the shades. Maybe some big-ass black bear has wandered down the mountain.

But what I see causes me to jump back in surprise.

This is no bear. Not even a cub.

I pull open the front door—shit, the only door in this one room cabin.

"What the hell are you doing out in a snowstorm?" I yell to the woman, Jameson barking behind me.

She's terrified, eyes wide and bright blue. Her hands clench a phone, using it as a flashlight, and her neck is wrapped with a hand-knit white scarf.

"I ... I ... I'm lost," she says, melting in a pool of tears out there in the snow. She's gonna freeze to death if she keeps crying. Ice crystals are gonna streak her cheeks.

"What the hell are you doing? You some crazy-ass fool?" I ask.

"No. I'm just. Really. Really. Cold."

I run my hands through my hair, trying to assess the fucking situation.

"Come in." I pull the door open wider, not wanting some woman's death on my back. And fuck, this woman is beautiful. Looks like a motherfucking doe in the snow-covered forest. Innocence and purity, her cheeks rosy red, her eyes a glistening blue.

"Thank you." She steps inside, not bothering to stomp off the snow she's carrying with her. This girl has no clue where she is or what she's doing. Grabbing a heavy-duty flashlight from the shelf by the door, I scan it out over the road.

In the far distance I see the outline of a vehicle. A small one. A fucking hatchback.

"You drove through the Idaho State Forest in January in that piece of shit?" I ask, confused as to why this mild creature would be alone out there, at night.

"In that piece of what?" she asks, disoriented. She spins, taking in my cabin, and when she does I see that beneath her fitted parka is a round little ass and curvy hips. Her blonde hair spills over her shoulders, nearly hitting her narrow waist.

"You drove that tiny car in the snow. In January. Whose dumb-ass idea was that?" I ask.

She may be gorgeous, but she made a few terrible decisions.

“Mine?” she asks, shoulders scrunched up. “I didn't think it was supposed to snow until after I made it here. But then I stopped at Starbucks, and had to run into Safeway for some groceries, but they didn't have the soup I like so I had to go to another store ... and the next thing I knew the day had slipped away.”

“Where were you headed, exactly?” I ask, wondering who let this naive woman out of their sight. This pretty thing is gonna get herself killed in the woods, the way she's going.

“I'm going to my uncle's cabin.” Unzipping her coat, she continues. “It's around here. I know it must be really close. I just didn't bring a paper map, and didn't exactly think through the fact that my phone service was going to cut out.”

“What *did* you think through?” I bolt the door shut, knowing she is staying put. Sure, I swore off the city, but I didn't swear off women.

I watch as she tugs her jacket off, revealing a perfect pair of tits. Fuck, this girl is porn star material. Perfect DDs pushed together, taunting me in that V-neck sweater.

“It's really hot in here,” she says, fanning herself, looking at the fire. “It's like a sauna.”

“It's not that hot,” I say, though I know she's

fucking right. The heat level increased the moment she walked through the door.

"Anyways," she says. "I thought through enough. I just didn't realize I'd get stuck. Can you help dig the car out so I can get to the cabin?"

"You crazy?" I scoff at this woman. I've met so many like her before, not thinking through a goddamned thing. Not realizing the implications of their requests. Who the hell did she think she was? "You aren't going anywhere tonight."

She laughs. It's a soft and sweet laugh, no rough edges on her. "I need to get to the cabin. If you won't help, can I at least borrow a shovel?"

"I'm not giving you anything of the sort. Not in the pitch dark, just so you can get stuck twenty yards up the road. You're gonna need a tow to get out of that mess."

"Well, then, what am I supposed to do?" she asks, her eyes brimming with tears. "I'm sorry for showing up here like this. I'm such an idiot." She shakes her head, biting her lip "I can't do anything on my own. Luke was right. I'm like a little girl with no experience."

I pull back my shoulders, trying to get a read on this woman. She may not have a lot of life experiences, but she makes up for it with charm.

She fucking drips sweetness. I want to lick her like a goddamned honeypot.

"Hey, no tears," I tell her, trying not to sound gruff. I don't have experience with relationships—I like to fuck fast and dirty, then move on to the next conquest—but I know enough to not be a complete dick when a woman cries. "Seriously. They are a fucking waste of time."

I watch her flinch at my words, and her tears start flowing more freely.

"I mean, it. You've gotta fucking stop with that. You aren't a little girl. You're a goddamned woman."

"I don't know about that."

"There are two things you need," I tell her, my arms crossed, my mouth twitching.

She looks at me all wide-eyed and innocent. Her chest heaves as she takes a deep breath, trying to control her crying.

"First of all, you need to get comfortable with the idea of sleeping here tonight, because you are."

I watch her look around the cabin again, her eyes landing on the two chairs next to the fire, on the table set for one. Her eyes wander to the ladder leading to the one-bed loft.

"And what else?" she asks. "What else do I need?"

"You need to calm the fuck down."

Her lips part in a smile, and—fuck me now —her face lights up this room.

"Why are you smiling?" I ask, realizing this woman is the opposite of the women from my past who were greedy and gluttonous, just like me. This woman is a goddamned angel.

"Today my motto was *Keep Calm and Carry On*," she says. "And then my car got stuck and I prayed for a miracle. I saw the smoke from your chimney, and it was like you were my savior. And now you just said my motto ... albeit a bit more garishly ... but my motto nonetheless. *Calm the Eff Down.* I can do that."

"What else can you do?" I ask, knowing exactly what I want her to do. I've been in the forest for two months, and I'm ready to fuck. I want her to spread her legs and I want to get her wet with my hard wood.

But she doesn't show me her pussy. Yet. Instead she sticks out her hand and says, "I can introduce myself. I'm Harper. And I'm so happy to have found you."

HARPER

The moment I set foot in the cabin I feel like my prayers have been answered. I know, it might be a little dramatic. But the entire time I stumbled through the snow to get to this cabin I prayed that it would be safe, and warm and not, like, the cabin of an axe murderer.

Sure, this man appears a bit intense. His flannel is unbuttoned, revealing a chest covered in tattoos, and he's strong and built like a man made for the outdoors. Broad shoulders and big hands.

And when he turned to bolt the front door shut, I couldn't help but sigh internally at the sight of his perfect rear in those worn jeans. Even though I know it's wrong to lust after a man.

But I'm not scared of him, or this place. He has furniture where it belongs, and everything in his cabin appears clean. Not at all like him.

He looks dirty—not, like, needs to take a shower dirty, but dirty like the men my father warned me about. Dirty like a man who knows his way around a woman.

Not anything like Luke. I admit, every time Luke touched me with his clammy hands, I was slightly repelled about the idea of our impending wedding night.

I always felt bad for thinking it, but every time I imagined being carried across the threshold and laid upon my wedding bed, it broke my heart a little. I couldn't help but feel let down, to have saved myself for marriage to a man like Luke.

A man who didn't even know how to use his tongue to kiss me.

One look at this mountain man, and I can tell he knows exactly what to do with his body, where to put his tongue. He stands with arms crossed, sizing me up. I like the way it makes me feel when he looks at me.

Warm, all over. Tingling. Awake.

He uses words more crass than any man I've ever spoken with. I'm never around rough and tumble men. Just the men in my father's congregation.

Standing in this cabin, I feel a long way from church.

I'm sure this man thinks I'm an absolute fool. Showing up here, like I need rescuing.

But I do. I need to be saved.

CHAPTER THREE

JAX

I KNOW a horny woman when I see her. Fuck, I've seen a lot of them.

And sure, Harper is fresh, a woman who's never been tapped. Everything about her drips with innocence—but her eyes are dripping with desire as she looks me over.

I feel the same fucking way as I rake my eyes across her body.

"My name is Jax," I tell her.

"Just Jax?" she asks.

"Jax as in Jaxon. But nobody calls me that," I say.

"Okay, Jax...." She bites her lip as if she doesn't know what to do next.

"If you give me your keys, I'll hike to your car and get you your shit for tonight."

"And leave me here?" she asks, panic written over her face.

"Shit, woman, what's your problem? You running from someone?" I cock a brow at her, trying to figure her out.

"Not someone," she says defensively. "But maybe *something*. My fiancé just left me ... so yeah, I'm a bit vulnerable at the moment."

"Honey, don't you know you shouldn't tell strange men in the woods that you're vulnerable?"

"Why not?" she asks. Her eyes dance with light and I can instantly tell that, while she may be a sheltered girl, she's a playful one. That will be handy to remember when I fuck her tonight.

And it's gonna be wild. I've been alone in this cabin for long enough.

She peers down at her chest, looks up at me with her pale blue eyes, and then asks, "Why wouldn't I want you to know that I am vulnerable?"

Oh, fuck me, woman. I feel my thick cock get nice and hard when she opens her pouty little mouth and speaks with innuendo. I know where I'd like those lips of hers to go. Right around my hard trunk.

I think she'd like it, too.

"Your keys," I say, holding out my hand.

She gets them from her coat pocket and hands them to me. When she does, I resist the urge to just grab her hand and pull her to me. I want to take her by the waist and throw her over my shoulder and head up the ladder to my loft.

I can picture tossing her on the bed and spreading those legs and burying my head in what must be a perfect, untouched pussy.

I have before me a woman who has never been fucked, that much is clear.

"My stuff is all thrown in, kind of all jumbled together," she says. "So if you can just grab my tote in the passenger seat that would be great."

"Sure thing," I say, grabbing my coat from the hook by the door.

"Oh, actually, I need other stuff too. That tote bag is just my toiletries. None of my clothes. I don't know ... maybe I should go look for that other stuff? It's all a mess."

"Girl, you aren't going back out there in that snow. You can get your clothes tomorrow."

"Then what will I wear to bed?" she asks.

"How about nothing?" I say, pulling open the door. I have to get out of here before my cock explodes. I have so much fucking wood for that woman, the only thing besides her that will chop it down is the frigid cold.

I have to find a way to get her to warm me back up before the night is through.

I thought being a lone mountain man was enough, but maybe I was wrong.

HARPER

Oh, my heart. I've never felt the space between my thighs tingle in such delight. A wetness seeps into my panties as Jax walks out of the cabin, into the snow-covered woods, for me.

I need to splash cool water all over myself. I need that ache in my belly to be taken care of.

Maybe I'm just hungry.

I look over at the refrigerator in the corner, and know in an instant this craving has nothing to do with wanting to be fed.

It was to do with wanting someone to eat me.

Oh my gosh. I clamp my hand over my mouth, shocked at my own vulgar thoughts.

But I know it isn't the first time I've thought this way.

So many times I've asked God for forgiveness over wanting the things I shouldn't. So many nights I've laid in bed, imagining a strong, rugged man running his hands over me. Wanting to put my hands *down there*, wanting to rub my hands over my nipples, as I imagined a man doing the same thing to me.

But I've always refrained, practiced self-control. Repented for having such forbidden ideas about men and their parts.

Not that I've ever actually seen a man's parts. I've never seen a man naked, never seen a cock—a word I used in my own head after hearing rebellious girls at church camp talk about having sex and using the word cock in their descriptions.

I love the sound of the word. *Cock* implies something hard and dirty. It offers a fullness that a word like *penis* never could. Those girls had referred to their vaginas the same way, calling them *pussies*.

While I've never spoken either word aloud, I've imagined saying them. Of course, I'd never have been able to talk to Luke that way. He always spoke about *God's word*. Which, who knows if he meant any of it.

He ran off on me.

Gosh, I do not want to think about Luke right now.

I want to think about Jax.

Which I know is completely inappropriate.

I put my coat on one of the hooks by the door and yank off my heavy boots as gracefully as I can. Which is to say, not very.

When Jax walks back into the cabin, my rear end is probably the first thing he sees, as I'm bent over trying to tug off one of my boots.

"Need help?" he asks.

"Ugh. Pathetic, right?"

"Not pathetic. These kind of shoes are motherfuckers."

When I grimace, he asks, "What, you don't like a man who swears?"

"I just haven't been around many is all."

"What, your daddy a preacher or something?"

My face feels flushed and, when I shrug, Jax laughs.

"Fuck. Shit, I didn't know. No wonder you're acting like a lost puppy. You've probably never been off your leash."

As he says that his wolfhound walks over to him and nuzzles his leg.

"It wasn't a leash." I smile and shrug again. "More like a harness."

Jax gives a bigger laugh this time, setting down my bag and taking off his coat. Revealing that rock hard chest again.

"But they let you take off the harness to come to the woods in the dead of winter, alone?"

"It was necessary. And it's not my parents who kept me tied up so much as my fiancé. *Ex-*

fiance. My parents are decent, and knew a little time on my own was what I needed. I'm not a child; I'm a grown woman. They know I can take care of myself."

"Which is why you're in my cabin without any clothes to wear."

"Hey," I say, finally able to yank my boot off in a huff. "That wasn't intentional."

"Still, sometimes we make choices subconsciously because they're what we really want."

Every time he speaks, my body warms up a bit more. I've already taken off my boots and coat, but if he keeps this up, I think I'll be down to my panties in no time.

"I don't subconsciously want to be here without any clothing."

Jax runs his hand over his thick beard and smirks.

"Maybe it isn't so subconscious. Maybe it's exactly what you wanted to do."

"You saying you know what I want?" I ask, standing a few feet in front of him.

"I think I know exactly what you want."

I toss him a flippant smile. "Then I'm sure a gentleman like yourself knows I'm starving."

"Oh, honey, I'm no gentleman." He walks toward the kitchen and I trail after him.

"What are you then, Jax?" I ask as he lifts the lid off a Dutch oven, revealing a roast with potatoes and carrots. The whole cabin smells like rosemary and fresh pepper. Divine.

"I'm a bad boy—one you couldn't handle if you tried."

"You don't know what I can handle. I just met you about ten minutes ago."

"Maybe you're right. I didn't scare you off with my cursing or my tattoos or my axe." His eyes dart over the fire and land on the polished tool.

"You don't scare me at all."

Jax sets the lid back on the pan.

"Maybe you don't want to eat right now?" he asks, his eyebrows raised.

My throat tightens. Oh dear, this is getting a little too real, too fast. I don't know what complete indecency has taken hold of me, but I need to backtrack, ASAP. I need to get to neutral, God-fearing territory. I need to eat my dinner and say thank you and go to bed.

That. Is. All.

I watch as Jax tugs off his flannel altogether, revealing tattoos covering his arms, too. I want to inch toward him, examine each piece of art—but I know I can't. Actually, I could; I just don't trust myself.

I don't trust myself not to take his big hand and push it down the front of my pants.

Oh my goodness!

I must really be having a nervous breakdown about Luke leaving me.

I've never entertained the idea of having sex before marriage vows, and here I am wanting Jax, a perfect stranger, to undo me.

“It really is hot in here,” Jax says, walking to the fire and dropping another log on the already burning ones. “If you get hot, honey, just take off another layer.”

“I don't have anything under my sweater,” I say, knowing a thin lace bra is the only thing between this sweater and my bare skin.

“No worries. I know it can get real hot in here, though.” He tries to hide a smile, but he does a poor job of it. He unhooks his belt buckles, and rips the belt from the loops, then tosses it to the floor. It skitters across the wooden floorboards.

I drop my jaw, realizing his game. He's gonna create a sweat lodge in here, forcing me to take everything off.

I turn back to the food and lift the lid.

“Mmmm, smells good. I'm gonna eat.”

Jax saunters over to me, his body right behind mine, and he leans over my shoulder, looking at the roast. A hardness presses against my bottom and I have to force myself to step forward, step away from him.

What I really want, what my body impulsively desires, is to arch myself right into him. The hardness that I feel press against me drenches my panties.

I've never experienced so much wetness down there, and it forces me to clench the lips of my pussy tight, as if I am scolding myself for such ideas.

But as I clench the lips of my pussy, it only makes the desire grow. This is all so new for me, these mounting sensations. I've never had them once with Luke. Never had them in my life.

Now I feel like I am on fire.

Just like those logs burning in the fireplace Jax has stoked.

Instead of pushing himself back into me though, he backs off and reaches around me for two plates.

"Have a seat," he tells me, as he places the plates on the table. I do as I am told.

He brings the pot to the table and scoops some vegetables onto our plates, and cuts a few slices of the roast for us as well.

Before he sits down, he grabs two pint glasses from the freezer and then pulls the tap on a second, smaller fridge. He fills each with frothy, amber beer.

Bare chested, his jeans slung low on his hips, hinting at what is below, he hands me a glass.

I take it nervously.

"Cheers," he says, clinking his glass to mine.

"Cheers," I say, raising it ever so slightly but not taking a sip.

He takes a long swig, and eyes me warily when I don't follow suit.

"It's the good stuff, I swear," he says. "I made it myself."

"I believe you, it's just ... I've never had a drink before."

"You've gotta be shitting me," he scoffs. "Wait, let me guess. It's against your fucking religion?"

"Yes," I say defensive. "My family isn't super uptight or anything like that, but we don't drink alcohol. And I don't really mind. I've never felt the desire to go against my father's wishes. Or even been in a situation where it was offered."

Jax sets down his glass, nearly empty.

"How old are you?" he asks.

"Twenty-one, why?"

"Just checking. I've never met a woman who hasn't been to a bar."

"Why would I ever go to a bar?" I ask, picking up my fork and spearing a potato.

"To meet a man like me."

"Then why are you alone in a cabin in the woods and not in some swanky bar in the city, with other hipsters, drinking fancy beer?"

"I'm not a hipster," Jax says, but his artisan

beer and beard and flannel say otherwise. When I laugh, he fake-glares at me. "That is a low blow, Harp."

"Already with the nicknames, Jaxon?"

He smiles at this, and it warms me up again. Not the heating up between the legs warmth—something comforting and safe.

"To answer your question, I don't go to bars because this is my home now. I used to live in the city, but I'm done with that scene."

"Why?" I ask. "What in the world could make a man like you decide to come out here?"

His eyes drop to his plate, and I can see that he isn't ready to open up to me.

Not like that.

But oh, my heart, I'm ready to open up to him.

I know it's wrong, but as he looks down at his plate, all soulful and full of a past I know nothing about ... I can't help but wonder if maybe tonight isn't about either the past or the future.

Maybe it is about being present, waking up tomorrow a new person.

Maybe I can *Keep Calm and Carry On*, by letting go of the one thing I've held so tightly to.

My virginity.

CHAPTER FOUR

JAX

SOMETHING HAS SHIFTED in the room when I look back up, and into Harper's eyes.

I can tell her mind is working in overdrive.

I don't want her to think at all.

We finish our food in silence. But she's mostly pushing the food around her plate and then looking at me, blushing, and then looking away.

"What the hell is going on, woman?" I ask her, hoping her answer will be what I want it to be.

She sighs, then drops her fork.

"It's just getting so hot in here," she says, breathlessly. "I think you were right. Maybe I should take off some layers."

"I thought you said you didn't have any layers," I answer smugly.

"I was wrong. I have one layer under my sweater. I have on my bra." She swallows, looks down at her chest, as if this is the dirtiest thought she's ever had in her whole damn life.

Fuck, maybe it is.

And maybe the things I want to do with her are the dirtiest things I've ever desired.

And that is saying one hell of a lot.

"Well, do what you need to do, honey," I say, pushing away from the table, my legs kicked open, my thumbs hanging on the loops of my pants.

"Oh, I know what I need to do, Jaxon," she says. She stands and walks to the fire. Her back is to me as she reaches for the hem of her sweater. She pulls it over her head in one fell swoop.

My hard cock is aching for her to turn around, to reveal herself to me.

I want to see her big beautiful breasts exposed.

Above the waist of her pants is bare skin and then the band of her bra. I want to snap it off her. Lick her from her nipples to her pussy and back again.

But first I want her to turn around.

"I've never done something like this before," she whispers into the fire.

Harper is different from the women in my past. Sure, those women were strangers, just like Harper. Just like her, they were looking for something with a desperation, a need—a hunger for my cock to satiate them the way only a one night stand can offer.

But Harper is nothing like those women.

She isn't experienced, has never been filled the way I intend to fill her now.

I moved to the woods because I needed to get away from everyone. Once the Sherriff started screwing with our business, I knew there was no point in sticking around. I thought that taking my money and moving out here, to the woods, would be enough.

But I was wrong. Nothing will be enough unless I can have Harper.

Not forever—I don't do that bullshit. But one night? Yes. One night is something we both need.

I walk over to her at the fire, my cock aching with each step I take.

"I'm so nervous," she admits, still not turning around. "I was going to save myself for marriage. But maybe...."

"Maybe you were really just saving yourself

for me," I growl, placing a hand on her shoulder and spinning her to face me.

Her eyes are filled with desire, with longing. I can't wait to fill everything up. And I know I will. Just as I guessed, she's a virgin. And her tight pussy is gonna explode when I set her down on my thick wood.

She'll never be able to walk again without thinking of my cock inside of her.

Looking down I take in her perfect round breasts. I want to take off that bra so I can see her nipples, so I can run my hands over them, massage them, suck them as she sucks me.

"Are they okay?" she asks, looking down at her breasts. "I've never taken my shirt off for a man before."

A smile dances over her lips.

"I did take off my top once with my fiancé," she adds. "I was trying to see how far we could go before he made me stop ... but he wasn't a man. He was nothing like you."

"So he's the one who wanted to stop before?" I ask, surprised. "Not you?"

"Does that make me slutty?" she asks. The word on her lips shock me. Everything about her has been so sweet and sincere—a word like that sounds so crass.

I like it.

"Wanting to make love is not slutty. It's natural," I tell her.

She bites her lip, her eyes dancing with the light of the fire. "I don't want to make love."

"What do you want?" I ask, lifting my hands to her chest, palming her beautiful lace bra. I want to pull it off, reveal her fully, but I want to take it slow, too, since it's her first time.

"I want to be fucked," she says.

I grin, unable to suppress it. This girl is making me insane.

She has been sheltered, but she wants to be set free.

I can unleash the collar around her neck, show her how to be wild.

It's what I've practiced my whole goddamned life.

I slide down the straps of her bra, using my fingers to unclasp the back. It falls to the floor, and her breasts tumble out.

"Fuck, your breasts are gorgeous."

"Don't call them that," she says, shaking her head adamantly. "I want you to call them tits. I want you to use the words I've never been allowed to say."

"Your *tits* are fucking gorgeous, Harper," I tell her truthfully. Because they are. They are the most gorgeous tits I've seen in my life.

"I'm glad you like them," she says earnestly. "Now ... show me your cock."

HARPER

I can't believe this is happening. It's the one thing I swore I would never, ever do before I was married.

The one thing I've imagined doing for so long.

And now I've taken off my bra ... or, rather, *Jax* has taken off my bra.

I never even got this far with my fiancé.

But Jax is nothing like him.

Thank you, God.

And now I lick my lips in anticipation. I have never seen a cock in my life. Not even a picture, not in a movie—because of course porn was beyond off-limits in my parents' house.

But I have imagined them.

I heard them described by those girls I went to camp with when I was a teenager. But since I finished my homeschool education and graduated, I've never spent enough time away from the house to be exposed to anything forbidden.

I helped my mom with my younger siblings, all nine of them. I never moved out because I was waiting to be the wife, the helpmate to Luke.

Before he abandoned me.

And the thing is, I wanted the life I was supposed to have with him. Simple, domestic. I still want to have babies, be a mother, home-school my kids, and make dinner for my husband. I just don't know when I will ever trust the men in our congregation again.

What if the other men who want to court me are like Luke? What if they end up being liars?

I can't think of that, because that is the future. And when I decided to take this one night as something for myself, I said I wouldn't think of the past or the future.

Just the now.

Keep Calm and Carry On.

"You are gonna love it," Jax says, unbuttoning his pants, not at all insecure. Not like me.

I'm so scared I'm going to do it all wrong, have bad sex and not give him what he needs. Because I know that's what sex is about—giving a man the thing they desire. At least that's all I've ever been taught in regards to my wedding night.

"I've never seen one before," I admit in a whisper.

"Well, honey, this is gonna be a fucking treat." He drops his pants, pulls at the band of his boxer briefs, and reveals his cock, in all of its naked glory.

I gasp, not able to contain myself.

"That is so pretty," I tell him, my eyes growing wide as I take it in. His cock is a hard rod, easily ten inches. The thickness is more than I imagined. I thought I'd be able to put my hand around it easily, but this is much bigger than that ... bigger than....

Oh my gosh, how could that fit inside me?

"Pretty?" Jax laughs. "My cock has been called many things, but pretty is not one of them."

"But it is, Jax," I say, reverently, dropping to my knees, wanting to get a better look. The color is a warm red, veiny and translucent in a way that gets my pussy wet. I've never imagined having such an irresistible desire to put my mouth on something.

But I do. I want that cock in my mouth, I want to feel it hit the back of my throat. I want to gag on his size.

I don't even know where these thoughts are coming from, but I am overcome by them.

"Can I touch it?" I ask, apprehensively.

"Oh, honey, you can do anything to it you like."

"Um," I say, looking up at him. "I won't hurt

it, will I, by touching it? It looks like it's about to burst."

"That's because you are the most fucking gorgeous woman who's ever laid eyes on it, Harper. That's because all I want to do is put my hard wood in your pussy."

I feel myself tremble at his words; they are the only words I've ever longed to hear. He wants me. Wants me hard and good. He wants me, and he is ready.

I take his length in my hands, slowly rubbing up and down, and he groans as I touch him.

"Oh, honey, that feels so good."

"Have you had a lot of woman touch you?" I ask, worry rising up in me again. I'm scared the other woman will have done it right and that I'll do this wrong.

"It doesn't matter. What matters is that you're touching me now."

He puts my worries to rest, and so I pull my hand up and down on his massive hardness, and then I reach for his balls. Two delicious balls, and I can't help but press my face closer to his rod, I want to smell his cock, his balls, all of him. He smells woodsy and clean. Pine needles and a wood stove. He smells like the Earth.

He smells like a man.

He moans as I do this, which makes me think maybe I am doing it right. His soft skin is like butter and I can't help but run my tongue down the length of him.

I have a desire to touch myself, but I push the idea away, knowing it is a sin to think that way.

But this is all a sin, isn't it?

I can't help but wonder why a sin feels so good? My tongue licks his cock, and I open my mouth wider, wanting to put his length inside. His cock pushes my lips wider, and his hardness fills my mouth, just like I wanted.

"Oh, Harper, that feels so fucking good."

I can't help but moan as I dip my head up and down, sucking on his rod. He thrusts into my mouth, and then puts his hands on my head, rocking into me nice and slow.

He groans and I fondle his balls with my hands.

"That's so nice," he says.

I love the sensation of his warmth in my mouth. It makes me feel so amazing, special. My hands and my mouth are making him so happy. I want to pleasure him this way all night long.

Before I can think that through, I feel his seed in my mouth. He thrusts harder in my mouth as he comes. With a rush of pleasure, I realize I get to swallow his come.

I pull his thickness out of mouth, wanting to see the come spurt from his tip. I've never seen such a powerful thing. Ropes of come are released, and I lean in to lick it off, to swallow the salty goodness. The powerful seed. I don't want any of it to spill on the ground—I want it in me.

I want him in me.

The realization fills my core with desire. I want that massive rod to press between my legs and I want that come to shoot up inside my pussy.

"I need more. I need more of you. Can you do that again, stay this hard and come again?"

"Oh, girl, I can come all night long."

"Then do that. Do that to me."

I stand and unbutton my pants, slide them off. Any of the inhibition I still carried left the moment I tasted him.

I want more of that creamy sex.

"God, woman," Jax says, grabbing my ass and pulling me toward him. I'm still in my panties, but I can already feel his hardness rubbing against me. It feels so nice.

I didn't think bodies could feel this way, and my pussy hasn't even been touched yet. Been touched ever.

Nothing has ever rubbed down there—not even me, because I knew it was wrong.

But now it's all I want.

Now it's so right.

CHAPTER FIVE

JAX

SHE IS A GODDESS. No question about it.

She tugs off her pants, and I wrap my arms around her, wanting to feel her skin, her soft curves, her enormous round tits pushed against my bare chest.

She sucked me off like I was a god, like she had never seen or tasted something so perfect.

Watching her lick up my come as I got off got me hard once again, instantly. My cock never had a chance to get soft, because how could it when a woman this perfect was running her hands over the length of me, in complete awe?

She fondled my balls like they were golden orbs. Like they were precious stones—and, fuck, it's good she thinks this way. My cock *is* a fucking treasure.

"I'm gonna fuck you so hard, Harp," I growl in her ear. "So hard you won't even remember what being a virgin felt like."

"Good," she says, already panting. "Why would I want to remember anything besides this?"

I lift her by her ass and carry her to the bearskin rug by the fire.

I place her gently on the soft fur, and then hungrily take in her perfect body. Cascades of blonde hair tumble around her, her tits rise and fall with each bated breath she takes. Her tummy is smooth and soft, the indentation of her belly button perfect.

Everything about her is so pure, even those little white panties she wears.

I'm on my knees before her, my bulging cock in her line of sight, just the way I know she wants it. Her knees are pressed together, because she has no fucking clue what is in store for her.

I tug on her panties, pulling them off, over her knees, past her feet. I throw them aside.

She bites her lip.

"Do you want me to stop?" I ask, not wanting to defile her virginity if she has changed her mind. I watch as her eyes look back down at my hardness, my solid wood that is sticking straight out toward her.

"You can't stop. Please. I want this so badly it hurts. Literally hurts, Jaxon. Like, my pussy aches. Is that normal?"

"Oh, honey, it's normal for women once they've seen my cock. This gift is not something every man can offer. It's what only I can give. And you are gonna fucking love this release."

"Then don't make me wait. Take me out of this agony."

I smile at her, unable to contain my mother-fucking grin.

I push open her legs, wanting to reveal her pussy. I want to see what I'm gonna be working with all night.

"Oh, fuck," I say, biting my lip.

"What? Is something wrong with it? No one's ever seen it ... or touched it."

"Not even you?" I ask looking at her nice, tight mound. "You've never touched yourself?"

"No, I was taught that it was a sin."

"Well, honey, tonight you aren't going to hell. You're going straight to heaven."

Her pussy is perfect, neatly trimmed and with folds begging to be parted. Her lips are pink and rosy, the downy hair so soft and fine.

She arches her back as I keep her knees apart, the vulnerability setting in, but I can tell she has pushed away any fear or hesitation. She wants this bad.

I use my hands to push open her folds. I see her tight little pussy so wet and lush, like a blossoming flower full of nectar.

I need to taste her. I lean down to her opening and let my tongue glide over her. Up and down her wet pussy, teasing her. I flick over her opening, knowing that her clit is going to be a motherfucking treat.

She tastes so sweet, her wetness dripping out as I move my tongue up and down, driving her crazy. My thick tongue fondles her tight slit as I lick her opening, and she moans in pleasure.

She's loving this, and I plunge my tongue in her deeper, sucking her clit, licking her lips until she is panting.

She starts to quiver and I lift my eyes, staring straight at her.

She screeches in shock, writhing her hips back.

"Oh, gosh, Jax, this is too much. Something's wrong." She grabs hold of my head and I see the sudden and unexpected fear in her eyes.

"Honey, nothing is wrong," I say, not having any clue what she doesn't like about this. I know how to work a motherfucking pussy.

"But it feels like my insides are going to explode."

"That's called an orgasm. And, honey, that's just the tip of my tongue. Just wait until my cock fills you up."

"That's an orgasm? I didn't think women had those?"

I try not to laugh at her innocence, at the sheltered way she's grown up. How could I laugh at the woman parting her perfect pussy open wide for me?

"Orgasms are for everybody, Harper. And they are just as nice to give as to receive."

"Just do it then," she moans, her back arching in desire, as if heat is crawling all over her skin. "I can't wait any longer, Jaxon. I need the release ... the orgasm now."

I wanted to take it slow, press my hands in her wetness, tongue her nice and good until she squirted her come all over my beard.

But I won't keep this poor thing in agony any longer. She's like a feral cat in heat.

I'll fuck her until she can relax.

Then I will lick her pussy clean.

HARPER

His cock enters me.

It's such a tight squeeze, such an intense pressure as he widens my untouched opening.

I close my eyes, breathing deeply, trying to

get past the pain as his enormous length fills me in a way I've never really understood.

"My God," I say, shocked at the way the blasphemous word escape my lips so easily.

"Oh, honey," Jax whispers as he leans over me, his tattooed chest hovering above me, his inked arms cradling me.

It hurts at first as he presses himself in.

But then it's as if I've died and gone to heaven.

JAX

I've had a lot of pussy in my life.

But nothing like Harper. I don't want to hurt her. She's so tight and narrow. I ease myself in as gently as I can, my hungry cock loving how tight she is.

But her eyes have sealed shut, as if she's wincing at the pain, and I feel horrible. Like a complete ass.

Then, she opens her baby blues, completely washed in ecstasy, and any feelings of remorse evaporate.

She looks so goddamned happy.

"Jaxon, this is everything." She smiles, shaking her head, biting her lip—a thousand emotions overcoming her at once.

"Yeah, it fucking is," I tell her as I press my hips against her milky flesh.

"I didn't think—"

"Don't think," I say. "Right now, just enjoy."

My cock fills her warm pussy and I know I've never had such sweet honey wrapped around me in my fucking life. Her walls press so tight against my rod.

"You like that, Harp?" I ask, running my hand over her breast, pulling her puckered nipple into my mouth. Sucking on her as she moans in pleasure.

I realize I haven't kissed her mouth. It's a shock actually—I'd have thought a girl as pure as her would want to make out first, but not Harper.

She went straight for my hard wood and hasn't let it get far from her sight since. Now I press my trunk in her opening, as wetness seeps out of her folds. I don't even need to touch this girl's clit to get her off, because as I grind against her, she is coming undone.

"Jaxon, it's making me crazy, it's making me —" She stops midsentence, but I don't.

I fuck her good, moving harder, faster, thrusting into her with the force that she needs. She was begging for a release and I am going to fucking give it to her.

She moans, she just fucking lets out the

most adorable, high-pitched wail as she grabs hold of my back, staring at me headlong.

"Thankyouthankyouthankyou," she cries as an orgasm erupts through her. Her body shakes, she tries to catch her breath.

I see a tear escape her gorgeous icicle eyes, but there is nothing sharp about Harper. Nothing cold. She is a pool of water and I want to swim in her again. And again. And again.

"Don't thank me," I tell her, brushing a strand of hair from her face.

She doesn't answer with words; she just takes hold of my face and presses her lips to mine.

Her soft tongue tenderly explores my mouth. I can't help but grab her ass and the base of her neck, and roll her over so she is straddling me. I cradle her in my arms, loving how small and delicate her frame is, unclothed, unburdened. She fits perfectly.

I devour her mouth, inhaling her skin that smells of flowers and milk. Skin that tastes like honey. She kisses me hard and with passion, wrapping her legs around me. We kiss until our lips our swollen, our mouths numb.

I thought the fuck we just shared was memorable—but this kiss is everything.

CHAPTER SIX

HARPER

I THOUGHT we would fuck all night.

But after I offer Jaxon my virginity, we kiss until I can't stay awake any longer. He tenderly pulls a blanket over me, lying me back down on the bearskin rug.

I fall asleep next to the fire, warmth trailing my skin, on every surface Jaxon touched.

I'm exhausted, but also wondering how in the world this will be enough.

How will I walk away from Jaxon in the morning when he still hasn't nuzzled his bearded face in my pussy, hasn't licked me like he said he would?

When I haven't had him enter my body in ways I can only now imagine. From behind.

With me on top. Against a wall. In a shower. My mind dances with the no longer forbidden ideas of what sex might feel like in those places.

I don't know how one time with him will be enough.

I fall asleep, his dog Jameson curled up near me. I hear Jaxon step up the ladder to the loft, and I fall asleep.

A dog is barking. Someone pounds on a door. Someone runs across the hardwood floor.

I open my eyes. The blanket is kicked off of me, and I am naked before a dying fire. But with one blink of an eye, I remember last night, and warmth floods my skin.

"What the fuck?" Jaxon yells as he races for the door, swings it open.

I roll over to see what the hassle is, reaching for the blanket to cover me. Wishing I'd had time to move before Jaxon swung open the door.

Standing in the snow is the last person I expected—or wanted--to see.

Oh my gosh. I drop behind the coffee table, but I'm no fool. There is no hiding in this one-room cabin.

"Is there a young woman here?" Luke, *my ex-*

fiancé, asks before scanning the space. When he does, his eyes land on me. His entire face changes. In a flash, he is red with rage. "Harper? What in tarnation are you doing here, like this?" he bellows.

I swallow, the taste of Jaxon still on my lips.

"I got lost...." I say, knowing how foolish that sounds. Shame ripples through me, knowing that this is going to get ugly, knowing I'm ruined.

I've been caught naked in a bad boy's house.

CHAPTER SEVEN

JAX

I WATCH AS THIS MAN, this fucking stranger, looks at Harper with absolute disgust. His lips are twisted into a snarl as he forces his way through my front door.

Like hell he is.

"What the fuck do you think you're doing, man? Step off!" I push him back. No way in hell is he gonna get close to Harper with eyes full of rage.

"Did you defile her?" the man asks, his words seething.

"Defile?" I snort. "What year you living in? Last time I checked, a woman has the right to her own body. And I sure as hell don't need you storming into my home accusing me of anything."

Pushing him back out in the cold, I turn to Harper. The blanket I dropped over her as she fell asleep last night is wrapped around her; the innocent doe now looks like a deer in the headlights.

"You know this guy?"

Harper is curled in a ball on the floor, her face streaked with tears. She's shaking, and I need to understand what this stranger has done to upset her.

"His name is Luke," she says, and while her eyes are filled with tears, her voice is parched, as if the well of her heart has run dry. "He's my ex-fiancé."

Whatever words she says next I can't understand because she bursts into tears, hysterical about something I can't take in.

I turn to Luke, who's in a rage on my steps. He's a clean-cut, khakis kind of guy, like a vacuum salesman or some shit. Out here in the frigid cold, he's shivering in his fucking boots like a motherfucking pussy.

"Her family is worried sick," Luke says, raising his hands in anger. "She left yesterday and never called."

He shakes his head, runs his hands through

his hair, the anger mounting—and I don't fucking need to deal with this bullshit.

"They should have never let her come on her own. What have you done to her?" Luke yells at me, like I forced Harper onto my solid wood. Like I told her to fuck me, begged to pop her motherfucking cherry.

"*Done* to her? She was the one on her knees sucking me off. You think I forced her?"

"Ohmigosh ... stop, Jaxon ... just stop." Harper is hyperventilating, her whole body near collapse.

I can't stand to see her this way.

"Harper," I say, kneeling beside her, holding her arms, trying to steady her. Luke is still screaming, but keeps his distance; he's still on my front steps. He's probably too scared to come in here like a real man.

"I have to go," Harper says, pushing away from my hold, standing. "I've ruined everything."

"Ruined what?" I ask, standing too. I take hold of her hand, not understanding, not wanting her to go before I do.

"I told you, my father is a preacher. Luke will tell him what he's seen, what you just said ... and they'll never see me the same way again. No man will ever want me now."

I laugh in her face, knowing that sure, she was an innocent girl walking in here last night, but really? She's scared that her dad is gonna find out she lost her V-card? She's a grown-ass woman.

"Don't laugh at things you don't understand, Jaxon." She bites back anything else she might say, and instead scans the room for her discarded clothing. She grabs her pants, the sweater. Her bra. I find her panties lying near the bearskin rug and hand them over as discreetly as possible.

I may like to fuck strangers, but I'm not a monster. The last thing I want is for a one-night stand to turn into a fucking fight.

As much as I wanted Harper again this morning, as much as I went to bed last night imagining all the ways I was going to fuck her silly today, I don't want to keep her here against her will.

I just need to get a better read on the pansy-ass at my front door. I need to make sure Harper wants to go with him.

Her face flushed with embarrassment, she mumbles, "I'm going to the bathroom to change, okay?" She looks up at Luke, shame washed over her once perfectly angelic face. It's as if she's seen a ghost.

"Harper, did you really fornicate with this ...

this ... animal?" Luke asks, as she walks away toward the bathroom.

Harper whispers to me as she moves to close the bathroom door. "Can you make him go? Tell him I'm coming, but I can't have him see me this way."

I nod. "You really want to go with the guy who walked out on your engagement? You feel safe with him?"

"I don't want my father coming up here, looking for you, Jaxon," she says quietly, pulling the door nearly closed. "Luke is gonna tell him what he saw here. I don't want you in my mess. I'm a big girl. I can pick up the pieces of my own life."

"You sure, Harp? I can't have you going with a man I can't trust."

"Luke is harmless. Obviously, he doesn't love me, but he isn't going to hurt me—like, in ways besides breaking my heart."

Tears fill her eyes again and she shuts the door.

I exhale. Fuck. This is not how I intended this morning to go.

"You're a sinner," Luke spouts off from the front porch. "And you've brought Harper into your debauchery,"

I'm a little relieved he isn't the sort of bible-thumper who calls unwed women names for having sex. Still, his words turn the cabin air stale.

Fine, blame me.

Heaven knows I have plenty to atone for.

"I think you should go," I tell Luke, grabbing my flannel shirt that I draped over the couch last night. I managed to pull on a pair of jeans before I crawled down the fucking ladder, but I kinda wish I hadn't. If my cock were hanging out for him to see, he'd know what a threat I am.

I know, it's bullshit, to think that way, but man, this asshole has me riled up in a way I never am. It's not like I want Harper for longer than a night—I was overdue for a good fuck and she came in from the cold.

But my friend Buck was right: I've been out here all alone for long enough.

Maybe setting up some sort of weekly fucking is in order. Is that a thing? House calls to lonely lumberjacks?

Fuck. I'm losing my shit. I need to get this guy the hell away, so Harper can calm down before she goes back home with this loser.

"You need to get off my motherfucking steps," I tell him. "Now."

"Not unless I have Harper," he says, straightening his shoulders, as if sizing me up.

I laugh in his fucking face. He stands no

chance with me. I'm easily twice his size, my muscles ripped from the fact that I've been felling trees for three months straight with my own goddamned hands.

"I'm not fighting you for her," I say. "If that's what you're worried about, don't. I got what I wanted as far as she's concerned. And I'm not concerned about you at all. I just need you to back the fuck off."

"But Harp—" he tries.

I raise my hand to stop him. "Harper is getting dressed. You best get her things from her car and go." I grab her car keys from the hook by the door and toss them his way. He misses and they fall in the fucking snow. "And you're gonna need to get a tow truck up here for the hatchback. No way is that thing gonna make it down anytime soon. It's supposed to keep snowing for weeks."

Luke grabs for the keys awkwardly from the snow, and nods as he turns away.

"Tell her I'll be back in an hour. I've gotta haul whatever she packed into my car, and I hiked up to your place a good distance—couldn't drive this far up the mountain. I came here because your place is the only house for miles. I never thought I'd find this." His jaw is tight, and his fists are, too. But he walks away.

Good.

I bolt the door shut.

I know he hates me for taking what he once saw as his—Harper's innocence—but I can't worry about that. Luke's feelings, or Harper's apparently crazy-ass parents, don't matter.

Right now I only care about Harper.

I don't fuck virgins just to have them fall apart the next morning. I need to make sure that doe-eyed girl is okay.

HARPER

The bathroom smells of pinewood and soap and, while it's tiny, it has everything it needs. A single-stall shower, an efficient sink, open shelving revealing his brand of deodorant and mouthwash. Both organic. I smile. Jaxon isn't so rough and tumble, he's more than the bad boy he presents himself as.

I wonder what other things I'd learn about him if I didn't have to leave.

I use a washcloth and try to clean myself up with the hot water and soap, trying to push out the conversation Jaxon and Luke are having a few feet away.

It's strange—I thought I'd feel dirty, waking up naked in Jaxon's cabin. And of course I'm blocking out the stuff with Luke finding me naked, and my father finding out soon enough—

that stuff has to wait until I can think it through.

Right now I'm just realizing that I don't feel dirty at all.

I feel amazing. I feel awake.

I feel ... like one night was not enough.

I close my eyes, forcing myself not to cry.

Why is life so complicated? It's like, I want the thing I shouldn't have. Want it so bad it hurts. And last night I gave away the thing I shouldn't have offered ... and if I'd woken up full of remorse, well, that would make things easy. I'd repent. Beg for forgiveness. Walk away and never look back.

But that isn't what happened when I saw Luke out there in the cold. Nothing about him appeals to me in a way that makes me feel alive. Luke and my family and our church are full of good, wonderful things.

But nothing like the wonderful way I felt last night when Jaxon was inside me.

Nothing like the wonderful way I felt when his cock was in my mouth.

Those things made me feel alive.

What does that say about me? I don't think I want to know.

I shake my head. This has to stop. This whatever is going on here, my quarter-life-crisis or whatever, is not gonna fly. Even if I wanted to, I can't have Jaxon again. My home, my family, my life, is in Coeur d'Alene.

Not in the woods. Not with Jaxon. He wasn't looking for a relationship last night; he was looking for the same thing as me.

A night full of passion—but passion with time constraints. Meaning, I should leave him be, let him get back to his beautifully tattooed, bearded-face, chiseled-abs life. Let him return to cutting down trees and brewing his own beer or whatever else a lumberjack does all day.

No way will my uncle let me stay at his cabin once he finds out what I did last night. I have to face the facts.

The South is not the only Bible-belt. My family is conservative; I'll be an example to my younger siblings.

I brush another tear from my cheek, still undressed. I need to hustle.

A knock on the bathroom door startles me. I'm still naked, but undone in other ways, too.

"Harp, you okay?" Jaxon asks.

"Is Luke there?" I ask.

"No." There's a pause. "Can I come in? We need to talk."

"I'm not dressed."

"Good."

My breath catches. Is this what I want? Jaxon to see me again ... take me again?

The answer is obvious. It wasn't even a question, was it?

"I need to know if Luke is gone," I say, my hand on the doorknob, already filled with hope that Luke has left.

"He'll be back in an hour. He went to get your stuff, but he's parked quite a ways back. Guess the roads are bad for a few miles."

"We have an hour?" I ask, swallowing. I look at myself in the mirror, noticing the curve of my hips, the way my waist narrows, the way my large breasts hit my skin, they hang so largely on my small frame.

I've never seen myself as a sexual being; wearing modest clothing and covering myself is a requirement in my household, and I've never questioned it.

But as I look at myself in the mirror—trying on the identity of no longer being a virgin, the one thing I've idolized for so long—I like what I see. Who I am.

I run my hand through my hair, trying to straighten it. It's no use. I let go and the long tendrils fall around my shoulders, fall in front of chest, my nipples poking out between the strands.

"Harper, you sure you're okay? I can't have the girl I took last night crying in my bathroom the next morning. It kinda kills my confidence."

"I'm okay, Jaxon." I open the door and step into him.

His hands rest on the doorframe, his open shirt baring a ripped stomach covered in black ink, in that criss-crosses his body, telling a story I will never have the privilege to know.

He reaches his arms around me, my bare skin pressing against him. He squeezes me tightly, not sexually ... even though that is what I'm gunning for.

"You sure you're alright?" Jaxon asks, his chin resting on the top of my head. I smile, liking the way I fit against him. "That was all a little intense out there with Luke."

"Luke isn't mean. He just didn't want to marry me. He said God told him we weren't right for one another. How could I argue with that?"

Jax snorts.

"Right, how can you fucking argue with God?" he asks.

Jaxon doesn't understand the weight of God's will in the place I was raised, by the people who raised me—my church family. God, to them—I mean *us*—is everything.

That's why after Luke broke things off, I kept moving forward. Sure, I needed to give myself space to heal—that's why I came to the woods in the first place. But I knew the breakup was okay if it was what God wanted. I know I can get through it.

Okay, and it also relieved me in ways I don't know how to quite admit.

I was never in love with Luke, and I doubt he ever truly loved me. If he did, he wouldn't have broken things off a few days ago.

"You want to go back with him?" Jaxon asks, pulling away so he can look in my eyes.

I must have been so overwhelmed last night with lust, because I never noticed the beautiful brown flecks filling Jaxon's irises. His eyes feel safe, and even though he plays it tough, I know he isn't only tough edges. There's a hidden softness to him, a softness I want. Now.

"I don't want to, but I need to," I say earnestly.

"Ever think of doing what you want?"

I smile softly. "Yeah." Shaking my head, I look to the floor. "But what I want doesn't seem very realistic at the moment."

"Take what you want, Harper. If even for a moment. Give yourself that."

"Is that easy for you?" I ask him. "To take what you want? Because it's never even been a option for me."

"Fuck, maybe I'm just a selfish prick, but why the hell not try it on for size?" Jaxon asks. "We have an hour. Take this hour and do what you want. No questions asked. Then when you go back to your weird-ass life with Luke or whatever, at least you'll remember what it felt like to—"

I cut him off, defensive. "I'll remember what it felt like to be alive." I look back up at him, feeling greedy and selfish, feelings I'm not used to at all.

Feelings that are spreading warmth throughout my body.

Can I really do this? Take what I want right now?

"You sure you're all right with me taking what I want, Jaxon? Because it pretty much involves your complete package."

"Oh honey, I'll give you my package."

The first smile I've had all day spreads across my face. "Your turn. I've already shown you mine."

I pull my hair back, standing before Jaxon completely naked, ready to take what I want.

Him.

CHAPTER EIGHT

JAX

THIS WOMAN IS TOO good for me.

I don't say that because I don't deserve to have a nice piece of ass give me a morning delight—but, fuck, Harper is just so damn pure.

She's almost too soft, too delicate to look at.

To take.

Sunlight from the window falls across her creamy skin and she looks like some goddess, her perfect tits perky and present, her shoulders narrow. Her body fit so perfectly against mine, but I think a person like Harper would fit against anyone. She would make anyone better by just standing next to them.

Her skin is completely unmarked—no scars, no stretch marks, no imperfections.

But God, this girl is scared. You can see it in her eyes—and, yeah, I joked about giving her my complete package and her taking what she wants, but I'm not a prick. I'm not interested in fucking a woman who is going to regret it.

And looking at Harper, her eyes swollen and her face streaked in tears, all I can think is that she must feel like a fallen angel.

But she has a long fucking way to go to lose her grace.

"I don't want you to regret being with me," I say.

I'd say something is wrong with me, because I've never spoken words like this in my life, but I know as a man it's the right fucking thing to do.

"You don't want me now?" she asks, blinking in confusion.

"Oh, honey, I want you. I just don't want you to go home and feel like you have to confess for the way I fucked you this morning. I don't want to be the reason your family disowns you."

"My family won't disown me," she says quickly. "I mean, I don't think."

"So you want this?" I ask.

"I do, Jaxon. I really, really do." Desire drips from her lips, and I don't need to be asked a third time to fuck anybody.

Especially not someone like her.

After ripping off my flannel, I unbutton my pants, slip them off. I don't have any boxers on and my cock springs up at attention.

"How do you want me to fuck you, honey? I know you must have been dreaming of it all night long," I say.

"I want you to take me to your loft."

I look over at the ladder, and smile. "Sure, but the ceiling is low up there, that gonna be okay?"

"That's fine," she says, another smile spreading across her luscious lips. "Because I kind of want to sit on you. That's a way to have sex, right?"

"Yeah, it is, and then you can sit on my fucking face."

She looks confused, and instead of explaining I pull her close to me and smack her round little ass. Cupping her breast with one hand I put my mouth to her firm nipple and suck it hard.

Licking her tits, I just want to massage them all fucking day long. I press my face in them and inhale the scent of her milky womanhood. My cock grows stiff with desire and I imagine her titty-fucking me soon enough.

I run my thumb over her lips, and then bring my mouth to hers. I kiss her hard, our tongues entwined as I make love to her mouth.

She's already moaning in pleasure, and I grab hold of her ass cheeks and lift her up. Her legs effortlessly wrap around me and her arms circle my neck.

"I'm so wet down there," she whispers, and her voice tickles my ear, causing a wave of pleasure to ripple over me.

I don't know if it's her talking about her wetness, or my wood already throbbing with readiness, but I carry her to the ladder and tell her to climb.

I want to be under her as she climbs those rungs. my face right under her pussy as she makes her way up to the loft. I can't help but run my hand between her thighs as she steps; she giggles softly, and my cabin has never been filled with such a sweet motherfucking sound.

She's as wet as she promised.

She climbs higher and her ass is in my face. I press my face to her cheeks, a hand wraps around her waist, and I kiss her perfect ass.

As she climbs higher I see her wetness drip down her leg, and I can't help but slide my tongue up the length of her, wanting her to take the final step to the loft so I can push her on the mattress, open her folds, and begin sucking on her juicy pussy.

"Jaxon," she moans, crawling over to the

mattress, and I trail her. "I want to touch you again."

"Of course, honey, I'm all yours." My cock is so hungry for her; I'm so hard and thick, ready for her to take me.

I lie on the bed and grin as she straddles me, my cock in front of her.

"Don't say it's fucking pretty this time," I tell her.

"But it is, Jaxon," she moans, licking her lips. Her nipples are so hard, I can't help but reach up and thumb them gently.

She holds my cock in her hand, then says, "Do I just, like, sit on it?"

I suppress a smile, loving the question, the innocence, the desire to learn.

Oh, I'll teach her.

"How about first you suck my cock," I say. "I know you're wet, but I want to get you nice and ready."

"What do you mean?"

"Turn around."

She leans her head to the side in question, but obediently turns, so her little ass is right in my face again. Like I want it. Like I need it. Her little pussy is ready to be worked.

"Now lean over, and suck me hard," I tell her. I grab her ass and pull her closer, wanting her to sit right on my face so I can lick every inch of her.

"Oh, oh my gosh, Jaxon, is this ... okay to do?" she asks as I hold her thighs, burying my face in her folds, just like I wanted.

"Oh, honey, trust me."

She leans over and my cock is instantly covered with the warmth of her mouth, her lips covering my hard rod, and she begins bobbing up and down. Oh, yeah, this is what I wanted to wake up to.

Not that fucker, Luke.

Knowing I'm the one with Harper on my face, not him, I'm anxious to make her scream so loud he hears. I want him to know that I can make her come, make her squirt.

I run my tongue over her slit, up and down, nice and slow, and I immediately taste the juice seeping from her pussy.

Oh, this girl likes a good licking. I dip my tongue in her opening, nice and deep, and she writhes above me; her sucking on my cock slows and she finds a pace we can both work with.

She bobs up and down on my cock as I flick back and forth against her pussy walls. Her clit is a nice round bulb that I want to run my mouth over all day.

But I have less than an hour, so I'll make the best of it.

I push her ass up a bit, my beard covered in her juice, just like I wanted. I want to get my hand inside her, finger fuck her hard, because I know she's never had that, never had fingers rubbing her clit nice and fast until she screams.

Oh, fuck, I want her to fucking blow.

She needs to. This honey pot hasn't been licked for twenty-one years. It's time.

Her cock sucking slows as she realizes that I am pressing a finger in her tightness.

"Is that your hand?" she asks.

"Just a finger. You can't handle a hand."

"Some women can?" she asks in awe.

I can't see her face, and I wish I could. I want to see her wide eyes full of wonder.

"Some women like a good fisting, but not you, Harper, not yet. Right now, I'm gonna go nice and slow, until you come all over me."

I love having her thighs around my face, her nice pink pussy right above me. I press two fingers in her, and move fast, up and down, faster and faster, and then use my other hand to rub in circles right at her opening until she's pouring all over my face.

This girl is a fucking waterfall, gushing with her pussy juice in a way I never get, because most women are too dried up for this kind of finger fuck.

But Harper is so tender, new. Untouched.

But she has been now—her back is arched, her moans increasing, louder and louder as she nears orgasm.

"Oh, Jaxon," she screams, as she moves to all fours.

I sit up, my fingers still inside her, pounding her pussy walls as she climaxes around them, tightening as she's overcome with ecstasy.

I motherfucking got her off and I know she loved every last lick, every single flick. She fucking loved me touching her, and now she's gonna take my cock.

HARPER

My body is covered in sweat, my insides wrecked in the most perfect way possible.

How am I ever going to go back to real life?

I still have a few minutes ... I hope.

"Do we have time?" I ask.

Jaxon's cock is still standing at attention. I loved having him in my mouth again, loved the way his thickness filled me, nearly taking my breath away. I took him deep in my throat, as deep as he could go, and still there was more of him. His cock was so big, so perfect.

I want him to fill my other opening now.

"We don't have much time, a few minutes," Jax says. "So I'm going to tell you what we're gonna do."

"What?" I ask, turning to face him, both of us sitting on our knees. The low wood-paneled ceiling slopes above us, and this small loft feels like a private oasis. Ours. And I know that's silly, I know this is a dream that is ending soon, and that when Luke drives me back home it will end in a nightmare—but right now I don't want to wake up.

Right now I want to stay in this fantasy with Jaxon, the fantasy that he has somehow brought to life. This bearded mountain man seems to know exactly what I need and has been willing to give it to me.

I must be greedy to take so freely.

"You're going to sit on my cock, just like you wanted."

Jason leans back on the pillows of his bed, his glorious cock standing so tall. I smile, completely undone by him.

"So I just kind of ... sit on it?"

"Yeah, honey, but nice and slow."

Jax holds my waist with both hands, and as I lean up, to try and position myself over him, I can't help but feel amazed that I am still here, having sex, with him. This gorgeous man with arms covered in tattoos, arms so ripped with muscles, and eyes that sear into mine.

And in this singular moment, he is mine. All mine.

He lowers me onto his cock. I hold the base of it as he settles me down.

"Oh, wow, that is so ... full," I say, not able to sit down on him. It's so massive and hard, and I can feel it stretch my tight pussy. I lean over his chest as I ease him into me. I'm still so wet and willing that my body eases any discomfort by lubricating his cock with my own juices.

"Oh, yeah, just move up and down, nice and slow," he says to me, his hands on my hips as I swivel around, completely filled with him. I can't help but moan as I fully relax into him.

"I feel like I'm going to orgasm just by sitting on you, Jaxon," I tell him honestly. But Jax moves my hips around, and I give in to the motion; the moment I do, I feel the way his cock hits my walls in a way his hand never could.

I feel my wetness pour out again as he rubs at my opening with his finger, nice and slow, in a circular motion.

"Oh, Harp," he says, his eyes closing in enjoyment. "That feels so fucking good.'

His encouragement excites me; I can't help but begin to move faster and, as I do, everything within me begins mounting in pleasure, building higher and higher as his cock rubs nice and good inside me.

He holds my tits in place, massaging them, and I love having his hands all over me, caressing me. I smile, loving the way my body brings him more pleasure. I want to pleasure Jax forever.

"I'm gonna come," he says, pulling me down, to his chest, as I continue to ride him. He cups my face in his hands and our eyes are locked.

In a make-believe world, in a world where I could actually do what I wanted, with whom I wanted, I would love to indulge in this fantasy. In my fantasy world, Jaxon wouldn't let me go after this morning—he would insist I stay, insist I stay in this very bed.

But real life isn't like that.

In real life, Jaxon is a sketchy guy, a guy who sees everything in a different way than I do, or my family does. In real life, Jaxon and I shared one night together, and it was never intended for more.

And as he looks in my eyes, his bulging cock filling me to my core, I know we come from two different worlds. Worlds where neither of us really fits anywhere besides the place we call home.

Still, he looks at me as we're both overcome,

moaning in pleasure as we orgasm in unison. My eyes fill with tears at the release, at the immense relief his cock delivered.

It was the best sex of my life.

Which, okay, it was also the second sex of my life, but oh, my heart—it was more than I ever imagined sex could be.

How can anyone preach against something that feels so good? So right, so natural?

I get off Jaxon, my heart racing, and fight to catch my breath. I fall to his side, his arm folding around me.

"No more tears," he asks.

"No tears," I say, wiping mine away.

"You gonna be okay, really?" he asks.

"What if I said no?" I ask, loving the way his fingers wrap around my long strands of hair.

"I'd say you should move out of your parents' motherfucking house and start living your own life," Jaxon says.

"Seems impossible," I tell him. And it would be. At home I have no money, a wedding dress hanging in my closet for a wedding that I'm not having, and siblings who need a role model. I can't just walk away from my life.

People don't do that unless they have a really good reason. And still, people don't just walk away from their lives. That would be too easy.

And my father taught me anything good in life is worth fighting for.

I can fight for my life, work to pick up the pieces I chose to break, even if it's going to be the hardest thing I have ever faced.

CHAPTER NINE

JAX

LUKE COMES BACK AS PROMISED. Harper has dressed, washed her face again. She says she's scared she'll smell like sex, and I try to be courteous and helpful. I make her toast and a cup of coffee to go.

I know, quite a stretch for a notorious asshole like me.

The thing is, Harper is different and I very well know it. I slept with a virgin—a nice, sweet, fucking goddess of a virgin—and I want her leaving my cabin feeling like her first time was better than she expected.

So I put butter and honey on her toast, and cream in her coffee, and make sure she is no longer crying.

I don't speak to Luke. What the fuck would I say? I fucked your ex-fiancée, and it was the best sex of my life—oh, also, her pussy tastes like the honey on that motherfucking piece of toast and she's pretty much ruined me as far as fucking is concerned?

I don't think that would fly with Harper.

"Thank you, Jaxon," she says, as Luke knocks on the door. "For not laughing at me or saying I was bad at it, even if I was."

I smirk. "Honey, I doubt there is a single thing you are bad at."

She shrugs modestly. "So, good-bye then?"

"You know where I am if you want to get stuck in the snow again."

"Bye, Jaxon," she says, as she pulls open the door, revealing a pissed-looking Luke. Surprise.

"Bye, Harper." I stand in my doorway watching her go

Watching her walk away.

She crosses the snow, and I stay put until she and Luke are gone from my line of sight.

As I move to shut the door, a deer runs across the snow, deeper into the woods. And I can't help but feel like it's gonna be a fucking long winter out here all alone.

HARPER

The car ride is torture. Luke lectures me for three hours. I don't cry, not once.

I don't know how to feel.

I can't feel bad for doing what I did with Jaxon. Our brief time together taught me one of the most important lesson of my life. A lesson that didn't come from the pulpit or a leather-bound Bible.

Sleeping with Jaxon taught me that being alive is a wild and precious gift I can give myself.

But I can never say that to my parents. How would I explain the ecstasy I felt sitting atop Jaxon's cock, that it made me feel holy and fulfilled? How could I explain that falling asleep in front of his fireplace, on that bearskin rug, made me content in a way I've never been in my life?

Those are things I will never tell a soul.

Those are memories I have to seal tight in my heart. I don't want to forget, but I know only pain will come from remembering.

As we pull up to my parents' driveway, I can't help but ask the question that I need to have answered.

"Why did you come looking for me, when you're the one who ended our engagement?"

Luke puts the car in Park and turns to look

at me. He hasn't calmed down since we left Jaxon's house, and I haven't tried to talk him down. What would I even say?

"Harper, I left our engagement because God told me to. God also prompted me to try and find you when your parents called. I care about you, we have a lot of history together—and, even if you are unclean now, at least you are home and can find your way back into the fold."

His words sound so strange ... did God truly prompt him to come look for me? And how could I find my way into the fold after last night? After this morning? I can't ask for forgiveness for the one thing in my life that felt so right, so pure.

Giving my virginity to Jaxon was an irreversible choice, and I would get on my knees for him all over again if I could.

"I can't go in there, Luke," I tell him. "My parents are going to kill me."

"No one is killing anyone," he says. "Want me to go talk to them first, alone?"

"No. I mean, unless God is telling you to," I say smartly.

"Not funny, Harper. What has happened to you? Twenty-four hours, and you're this completely different person."

"Well, it started with you ditching me a week before our wedding, Luke."

"It was God's will," Luke started again. "You aren't the right woman for me, I need someone more...."

"More what?" I ask, incredulous. Luke ended things with me so quickly that I couldn't even ask him questions to try to understand.

"More reverent."

"I didn't, what, pray enough?" I shake my head, so frustrated. I did everything by the book. I went to services three nights a week, volunteered at the food bank, helped my parents run the household. I had toilet-trained five of my siblings for goodness sakes. Yet I wasn't holy enough for Luke? "What are you looking for?"

"Not a girl who sleeps with dirty men in the woods," Luke says, his eyes narrowing in on me.

I have to get out of this car. Facing my parents will be terrible, but staying here with him, being humiliated, is worse.

Unbuckling, I grab my bags, sling a tote over my shoulder, brace myself for my father's wrath.

"I already called your parents and informed them," Luke says coolly as I push open the car door.

"Did you...?"

Luke sneers, suddenly a man I can't believe I ever considered spending my life with.

"I told them I found you naked in the house

of a man who claimed he'd had his way with you."

"That was my story to tell," I whisper. My eyes fill with tears once more.

I drag my bags from his car, not able to stand being there one more minute.

Standing on the front porch of the house where was raised, I knock the door.

My father answers, his face cold and stern.

"You have shamed us all." He berates me the moment I walk inside. He turns out the door, toward Luke's car and I don't say anything to him.

What is there to say? He runs this house and I have humiliated the family name.

My mother comes to the foyer, her eyes covered in the shadow of disappointment.

"What have you done, Harper?" she asks, shaking her head.

"I didn't—" I fall into her arms. "I never meant to hurt anyone."

And I didn't. I'm not going to apologize for last night, but no one else needs to be hurt as I try to mend what I have broken.

"How will you ever find a husband now?" she asks as we embrace.

"Mother, there must be more to life than that?" I ask, pulling away.

Some of my siblings walk through the hall—

James, Jonathan, Jessie, and Hope—heads bowed, not even looking at me.

"Hi, James," I say to my brother, who is two years younger than me. He's my closest sibling in age; there's a three boy, eight-year gap between my sister Hope and I.

James doesn't meet my eyes, and everyone walks to the schoolroom in the basement without a word to me.

"Why won't they look at me?" I ask Mother.

"You have disgraced us, and must pray for forgiveness. Your father has required this of all of us." She won't meet my eyes, and shame runs deep through my veins.

I can't reconcile what happened with Jax this morning, the absolute ecstasy, with that I feel now.

I see Father turning back to the house, and I can't bear his fury.

I take my things and walk to my room. Falling on my bed, I can't imagine ever bowing my head in prayer. Repenting for being with the bad boy, Jax.

I'm a fool.

A fool now stuck in a house where *I'm* the bad girl.

CHAPTER TEN

JAX

BUCK SHOWS up at my cabin, telling me I need to come down to the bar, and for some reason I agree.

It's been four weeks since Harper left. I never learned her last name, her home address. And of course I didn't. She was a one-night stand.

But she hasn't left my mind.

The snow has melted, the promise of spring finally poking its way through the forest floor.

As I follow Buck down the mountain in my own truck, I see a beautiful doe on the side of the road, her white spots pointing to her purity, her eyes alert, taking in the world as it passes.

Once again, all I see is Harper.

A tow truck came up the road a few days after last month's snowstorm passed. They carried Harper's little hatchback down the mountain and I knew that was that.

I could have been a creeper, gone all stalker-mode in her car, rooted through her glove box, looking for an address, a phone number. But I resisted. She didn't offer those things, and I could guess she'd gone back home to a family ready to lay it on her.

I didn't need to show up on her doorstep and get punched by an angry father.

I stayed put.

I'm no love-sick fool. We shared a night I'll remember, but that's all.

At the bar, Buck hands me a can of Bud Light and we play a few game of pool with the regulars. Some women ask if I want to go somewhere to talk, and while Buck thinks it's goddamned amazing having me as his wingman, I pass on the offers.

I'm not ready to get into something with some girl who lives out in the sticks. There aren't enough houses in these parts to keep my one night stands in order.

When I did that back in the city, it got me in trouble with the Sherriff. It's the reason I'm out here in the first place.

Better I keep my wood in my pants.

Best I not start in at all.

I help Buck with the women, though. That poor bastard has no game, and the least I can do is put in a good word for him.

Clapping him on the back, I explain his merits to some local girls. "Buck here has had my back for as long as I've lived here," I say.

"And how long has that been?" asks a brunette in a jean skirt and cowboy boots.

"About three months."

"You the guy living in the woods all alone, chopping trees all day?" her friend asks.

"That's me," I say, taking a long pull from the beer. "But Buck here isn't as sketchy as me. He lives in town, owns the gas station—and last time I checked he had some property out on the lake. Prime for camping. We should all go sometime."

"That sounds hot," the cowboy-boot girl says. "Like, so hot I'd have to take my clothes off." She taunts me by unbuttoning the top button of her shirt.

I don't take the bait. Instead, I think of how hot Harper got in my cabin, how she stripped to cool off.

How I'd strip her again if I got the chance.

How I'd never let her go again if I did.

Should have never motherfucking let her out of my sight. I should have fought for her.

Only thing is, she didn't want any saving. She wanted gone.

HARPER

I throw up every day for two weeks. I'm losing weight.

Losing sleep.

I must be dying.

I must be dead.

At least, this must be what death feels like.

I know people really are dying, and I understand it is callous and cruel to speak this way—but, truly, if there was any way I could get out of this life, I would.

I can't see it happening. I have no money, no experience. And in the meantime, I am getting myself ill. Sick over the prayer-fasting my father requires and the bible studies and the sex-addicts meetings in the church basement.

Yes, my parents thought I needed a twelve-step program for having sex one solitary time. Okay, two times, but they didn't know the details. Oh, they asked all right. But I refused to tell.

Apparently, they thought sex with Jaxon one night was a gateway drug.

They weren't that far off.

Because, oh my heart, I can't count the

number of times I've parted my legs in the dark, under the covers, and imagined him. His hard chest and harder cock and his fingers pulsing in my opening.

I just need a few minutes imagining him covering me with his body, and my fingers slip between my thighs, into my folds. I keep trying to take the edge off the way he could.

But nothing I do to myself feels anything like he felt to me.

I want to be in his cabin. I would ask him how he fingered so well ... beg for the magic secret. But there are a thousand reasons I'll never go back and ask Jaxon, and one of them being I have nothing to offer him.

Luke never called after the day he dropped me off. And good. I don't need to see him ever again. Last I heard, my father mentioned him going to Bible College in Denver.

Maybe he'll find a pious woman. A woman I can never be again.

"Harper, you need to clean up after breakfast," Mother says, knocking on the bathroom door. In the bathroom, I retch up my oatmeal, with the fan on, the faucet in the sink running.

Letting on that I'm sick would just be another way to drag out the consequences they've thrown on me.

I'm already on restrictions. My one freedom

is when I go to the Food Bank to stock shelves. Besides that, I'm at home 24/7 and pretty much useless.

I'm tired of being a little girl, of not knowing how to do things. So I am trying to be responsible. Prove my worth. The last thing I want is another guy like Luke not wanting to be with me because I wasn't enough.

Since I came home a month ago, when I'm not cleaning, doing laundry, helping with the dishes and cooking, I make myself scarce and try to rest. I'm always so tired.

But I can't be tired. I need to get up and start the day and show my family that my foray into the woods was a one-time thing.

It's not working this morning, because once again I'm sick. No matter how plain my food, I still get sick like clockwork

I go to the kitchen, begin rinsing oatmeal bowls and then eventually stacking the dishes in the cupboard.

Before I have to run out of the room.

And get sick again.

CHAPTER ELEVEN

JAX

THE SNOW IS GONE and I'm out back, an axe in hand. My shirt's off, beads of sweat falling off my back. It's motherfucking hot out here.

I went into town yesterday, checked my email and bank account. My parents emailed letting me know they were in Florida, in their RV, following their retirement dreams.

I'm happy for them, to have what they want. They say they worry about me, their only son. I emailed back, telling them I'm good. Great, even.

What they don't know won't hurt them; it'll keep them happy. That's what I want.

I saw the last deposit made to my account from my buddy Dean. It was twice the size it usually is. Guess the trucking company is taking off.

I swing the axe against the massive pine, my eyes burning in jealousy. Anger.

Guess he didn't need me to be his right hand man after all.

Even though it was my business plan, my love for these old logging roads and these mountains. My desire for people all over the country to have a piece of Idahoan pine and cedar in their custom homes.

Fuck that shit.

I take another swing, like a goddamned lumberjack, not sure what the point is.

I'm out here, because what? I'm being punished for fucking some Sheriff's daughter?

It's bullshit.

I don't want to be a part of a life like that. So rigid, full of rules. I don't live by the law of anyone.

I live by the law of the mountain.

I take a final swing, and then push against the trunk as the pine falls. I've been hacking at this beast for four hours.

Stepping back as it falls, I look around my property. I love this land. And fuck Dean. Fuck our company. Fuck it all.

I don't need that bullshit.

I pick up the shirt I threw on the ground

when I got hot, and wipe my face with it. It may be March, but I've worked up a sweat.

As I move toward the cabin for some ice-cold beer, my axe in hand, I see a small car roll up into my driveway.

It's the last fucking car I ever expected to see again.

It's Harper's hatchback, and she's alone.

She steps out of the car, her face streaked in tears, the same as when she left.

Has this girl been crying for six week straight?

"Harper?" I move toward her and we meet at the steps to my cabin.

"Hey Jaxon ... I hope it's okay that I'm here?"

"You okay?" I ask, shaking my head. She's wearing a long top over a pair of leggings, boots on her feet. Her long blond hair is braided over her shoulder.

She's effortless.

"I've been better. I didn't know where to go."

"Uh, okay, is it your family? That bastard Luke? Did someone hurt you?" I have a million questions for her. Flashes of our time together fill my mind.

Her bare skin, soft and milky. The warm

space between her legs. Her wonder, excitement, willingness at the night we shared.

And she's back. I want to pull her in my cabin, lock the door. Never let her go.

But she doesn't look alive with the hunger of desire.

Harper looks motherfucking exhausted.

"I don't even know how to say it," she says.

"Uh, you hungry? Thirsty?" I ask, trying to remember how to be polite to guests. No woman's been up here since our time together.

"No, I'm fine."

"Okay...." This is kind of awkward. I want to kiss her or fuck her, but she came here to talk.

"Can we take a walk?" she asks.

"You drove three hours to take a walk with me in the woods?"

"No," Harper says, sighing deeply, like this is all too hard. What has her so worked up? "But maybe if we walk it will calm my nerves."

I bury my ax in a stump and nod toward the path I usually walk on when I want to move my legs.

We walk past my piles of hewn logs, many covered with tarps but others still in the process of being stripped before I send them to the sawmill. Not that I have any motherfucking plan for all this wood.

"You cut trees?" she asks. "Like, is that your job?"

"Sorta." I shrug.

"Why don't you use a chainsaw?" she asks, curiosity dancing over her blue eyes. "Wouldn't that be a lot easier?"

"Easier, yeah, but the point isn't to do something easy."

"What is the point, then?" she asks. Her arms are crossed over the jacket she's now zipped up to her chin.

"The point is to simplify. Cut out all the crap, the bullshit."

"You want things simple?"

"Yeah," I say, not sure where she got confused. I'm being pretty damn clear, for a man. "I don't want drama. I want things easy."

"Oh." Harper stops on the path. We haven't even walked ten yards and already she needs a breather. "You know, Jaxon, maybe this was a bad idea. Maybe I should go."

"What are you doing to me, woman?"

Her eyes fill with tears. I swear there is nothing, no one, more fragile than Harper. It's like she can't stand on her own two feet.

"I'm sorry, Jaxon. I just ... I can't. This is too hard. Too much. I should go."

"You aren't going anywhere and we both know it."

She swallows, looking up. As she does, she gasps, points to something behind me.

I turn and see a deer family. A twelve-point buck, a beautiful mama beside him, a small baby deer between them.

"That's beautiful," Harper says.

"Sure is," I agree, knowing if anything is gonna calm Harper down, seeing these creatures will. Our eyes are still on the family, and we don't dare move, not wanting to scare them off.

I swear I can hear Harper's heart beating from where I stand. This girl is so worked up. I take her hand in mine, want her to feel safe. I mean, I'm not the poster child for security but, fuck, this girl came all the way out here to find me, didn't feel like there was anyone else she could turn to. Might as well not be an ass about it.

"Can you tell me what you're doing out here?" I ask her, as quiet as possible so as not to disturb the deer.

"It's bad, Jaxon." Her words are so delicate they nearly disappear in the air before they reach my ears.

"Nothing can be bad when we're looking at this," I say. The deer family stares us at, with the same curiosity we show them.

Her hand shakes in mine. I squeeze it, trying to calm her. It must work, because she opens her mouth in a whisper and says the words I never wanted to hear.

HARPER

This morning I already know the truth before I confirm it. I tell my mother that someone has called in sick at the Food Bank and that I needed to go help, right away. I lie right to her face and get in my car.

I drive three hours. Three hours where my mind is numb and my heart is numb and all I know is that I could never *Keep Calm and Carry On*. Not now.

Everything has changed.

I drive to Jaxon's cabin, praying to a God who seems to have left me a long time ago, left me to the devices of a church family who will never accept me.

Where else am I supposed to go?

Jaxon is right where I left him.

I park my car, my whole body on fire the moment I see him in the distance. His arms swing, axe in hand, as a massive tree falls to the ground. The heaviness of the trunk swooshing through the air takes my breath away.

It is so final, so swift.

It took so many years to grow that tree, and

then in a few hours it is chopped down to nothing. A fallen log with no life.

The same thing has happened to me, and the realization sends tears to my eyes. I spent twenty-one years working hard to grow into something beautiful and good and strong and sure.

And then one night, one choice, caused my life to crash to the forest floor, just like this tree.

Timber.

Jaxon's chest is bare, his beard a bit longer than I remember. The second I see him, I want to run my hands all over his skin. I want to fall into his arm, smell his earthy scent—the pine needles and wood stove smell of a man. I want him to carry me away from the nightmare that is my life.

It's as if when I came here before I entered a dream, and when I left I floated into a nightmare.

I want to go to sleep with Jaxon, in his bed, wrapped in his arms.

When I was with him, everything made sense, even though it was the opposite of everything I valued. Jaxon made me feel safe in a way no one else ever has.

But these thoughts shame me.

Have I learned nothing this month?

My actions have consequences. My family

still shuns me half the time, shake their heads in disapproval. The entire congregation knows about my lost virginity.

I am a used woman.

And now, the moment I see Jaxon, all I think is that I want to be used again. Over and over.

But I won't have what I want.

I owe him the truth.

He must be surprised to see me, but he doesn't show it. He looks worried, and I scan myself self-consciously, wondering if I look so different now than I did before, when I was undressed and offering myself to him.

I can't go in that cabin. I don't trust myself in there, so when he offers me something to eat or drink I shake my head. I suggest a walk in the woods.

We walk into the trees, and as we do it's as if we are sheltered by their branches, covered by their limbs.

I feel safe out here, with Jaxon, but I'm too scared to speak.

The family of deer calms my nerves, but the real thing that soothes my anxiety is Jaxon's hand on mine. He squeezes it tight, and I remember to breathe.

No one has touched me in six weeks, not

since that first hug from my mother when I walked in the door.

It's a part of my lesson, my father says.

I must tell Jaxon the truth.

I open my mouth.

My words hit the air with a force that scares the deer away; they startle, and run as fast as they can. Jax turns in shock, startled by my words, too.

"Jaxon," I say. "I'm pregnant with your baby."

CHAPTER TWELVE

JAX

I STARE AT HARPER. Her pale blue eyes are filled with tears, and I hate to see her this way.

I'll admit, hearing that she's pregnant gets me hard. It turns me on, knowing my powerful seed filled her. I remember her dripping pussy; I remember how desperate she was for my massive wood. A slow smile spreads across my face, remembering our time together.

But her wounded eyes bring me back to reality. I may have knocked her up, but this is a hell of a lot more complicated than two people in love making a baby and living happily fucking ever after. Harper and I are strangers, and the last thing I need is a woman hanging around for longer than one night—let alone her kid.

"Fuck, Harper. I did not see that coming."

"I know, Jaxon, it's too much. I can't even think straight yet ... but I thought you deserved to know."

I run a hand over my beard, trying to think of anything besides the fact that her jacket does nothing to hide her perfect tits, that her skintight leggings show me every curve on her body. That all I want to do is hold her against a tree and take her again, like we did in my cabin.

I want to take her all day and all night.

But she doesn't appear to be filled with the same sort of desire. She mostly looks fucking terrified.

"What are you thinking, Jaxon?" Harper asks. "I've been agonizing over this the entire drive here. Thinking about what we should do ... how this might work. My head hurts. I can't figure this out on my own."

"Well, shit, I don't want your head to hurt, Harp." I step toward her, cupping her cheeks with both my hands. Touching her stills my wild heart for a moment, but what I really want is to growl filthy words in her ear, devour her pouty lips and push my fingers in her opening until she screams my name.

What I really want is to pretend she didn't come here today to tell me I'm her baby-daddy, and instead act like she came out here ready to be taken hard and fast.

Her breath catches as I lean in to kiss her, but she doesn't push me away.

Her lips are sweet and I press my tongue in her mouth, tasting her as I run my hands through her hair, pulling her closer to me.

She looks up, into my eyes. "Shouldn't we talk?"

"You wanna talk right now?"

She shakes her head, her eyes close, and I can imagine this woman has had a fucking long six weeks, what with her screwed-up family and freaky fiancé. I'll make her forget all those worries for a while.

I unzip her jacket and tug it off. Lifting the hem of her shirt I raise it over her head, without saying a motherfucking word.

"Out here? Will someone see?" Harper is so fucking on edge, I'm taking it as my responsibility to get her to loosen up.

"Honey, no one's out here. Now let me fuck you. I know that's what you want. What you need."

She nods her head, ekes out the slightest moan, and I toss her shirt to the forest floor.

Her tits are as perfect as I remembered, but fuck me now, they seem to have doubled in size since I saw her last.

"They're swollen ... because of the ... well, because. Be soft?" Harper's inflection sends a chill down my spine. She's not like any woman I've ever met—she's more tender, more pure. She fucking needs a man to take control, and I will.

"Oh. I'll be soft with your tits, but nothing else." I pull down the lace of her white bra and then bring her perfect hard nipple into my mouth, suck it slowly, before moving to the other one. Harper's body is so primed for this moment. Her back arches in response; her legs spread subconsciously. "I bet you've been thinking of my massive cock for six weeks straight."

She doesn't answer, just bites her lip, hiding a smile. And I know she *has* been dreaming of it. Of me.

"You touch yourself at night?" I ask. "Remembering my wood, how it filled you up and made you drip?"

"I did, Jaxon," she moans as I press my hand down the front of her pants, under her soaked panties, fingering her soft folds. Oh, Harper has been thinking about my cock all right. Her pussy is fucking swollen with desire.

"Good, because I've been thinking of your pussy—how good you taste, how hard you got me—every day, too."

"I thought you had lots of women out here?"

"Naw," I say, shaking my head as I rub her clit until her head falls back in delight. "I don't bring women out here. I left that behind in the city. Out here, I've only had you. I prefer to play by my own fucking rules, be my own man. And most women don't understand that."

She wraps her arms around my neck, pulls herself closer to me, grinding into my stiff wood. "Fuck me, Jaxon. Out here, in the wild. I like you out here, untamed."

Her words fill me with confidence, not like I motherfucking need it. I know how well I fuck, but I like taking Harper. She likes to compliment, to tell me what kind of man I am.

Her hands squeeze my bare back; my solid chest is against hers. Stepping back, I unbuckle my jeans, tug them down, and reveal my hardness for her. She sucks in air, the same way she did before, and shakes her head as if she can't believe it.

"Oh, Jaxon, just looking at it makes me so ... so ...."

"Wet?"

"Exactly." She steps out of her shoes, pulls off her leggings and panties—and she must have known today would end in a good fucking, because her pussy is nice and trimmed, ready for me to lick her clean.

Her feet step gingerly on the grassy bank, but I won't let her get dirty. I lift her up at the waist, her legs wrapping around me. Massive pine trees surround us, the forest is full of birds chirping and water flowing in the creek. The deer family is long gone, but I am sure some critters are around here watching us. I fucking hope they are. They can watch and learn.

I press my cock into her opening. I know we got here fast, but it's chilly out here, and this woman is fucking pregnant. I'll take it nice and slow later, but right now what Harper needs is to be fucked silly, until all the stress and worry of her life at home are gone. Until her mind is filled with one thing, and one thing only.

My wood.

HARPER

Oh, my heart. My legs are wrapped around him, and his thickness fills me again. I think I might burst.

For the past six weeks I've tried to remember what it felt like to have Jaxon inside me. I even tried to recreate the sensation with my own hand ... but that was ridiculous. Because, I mean, I don't even know what I could use to actually recreate the size and force of Jaxon inside of me.

I sit on his cock, and he thrusts into me deep, then deeper. His hands stroke my ass as I bounce on top of him.

"Fuck me, Jaxon," I say, letting the forbidden words escape my lips deliciously. I have thought of this moment—me being with him again—so many times it made me dizzy. And now I have him inside me once more. I know I'm playing with fire, but right now I want to burn.

"You like that, Harp?" he asks, and I squeak out a yes, because that is the best I can do. The walls of my pussy are blazing hot—scorching really. It's an all-consuming moment as he pushes deeper into me once again.

And then I'm moaning as he fills me with his come, and I feel my own juice pour out, slick on his base as he slams me down on his hard cock a final time.

His insanely large biceps lift me off him, setting me on the ground. Holding me up as we fucked didn't even seem to faze him. He's so strong and capable. I'm out of breath, but he just grins like a beast—a man made to have sex in the woods. His bare chest and bare ass, his long beard and piercing eyes. He is an animal and I want him to take me like I am his prey.

"You want to come inside my cabin now, or are ya still scared of what I might do to you?"

Jaxon asks, pulling up his pants. I reach down to put on my own clothing, blushing as I do.

"I'm not scared of you," I say, adjusting my tender breasts in my bra, then straightening my top. I tell him I'm not scared, but I am completely terrified. I have no idea what I should do next—I just hope Jaxon will be willing to help me figure it out. You know, before I hyperventilate in fear of the unknown future.

"Good, then come in," he says. "Let's talk."

Jaxon opens the door, holds it for me.

I look around the cabin and see it for what it is. I didn't remember what it was like in the daylight. When Luke came here to find me, to drag me home, the morning was so dramatic, I wept as I left.

Now I can see the tiny cabin in the light of day. It's a complete bachelor pad. It isn't dirty or skeevy or anything like that, but it's definitely Jaxon's. I realize, not for the first time, that I don't really know anything about him, what he does out here besides chop wood like a lumberjack. I don't know what I'm expecting from him … I mean, besides fixing all my problems.

I sit down on a chair by the fireplace, and rock nervously. The bearskin rug is still on the floor, and I'm reminded of how I fell asleep there, curled up, feeling so safe and warm.

Looking around now, though, I'm not so sure if this place offers the same comfort I hoped it would.

Jax's big, loveable dog Jameson pouts at his feet until he relents and tosses him a bone from the cupboard.

"You hungry too?" he asks me, pulling the tap on his kegerator and filling a frosty glass with beer.

"Actually yeah. I'm starving." Which is true, but also the first time I've had an appetite in weeks. Looks like what I needed to get me hungry was for Jaxon to take me in the woods. "Let me help, though," I say standing.

Walking around the cabin, toward him, I reassess. Maybe I'm hungry here because I feel comfortable with Jaxon in the woods. Not sick. Not ill, like I do at home. Maybe this is the place I should be. I mean, would it be so bad?

The cabin might be small, but I could have this baby here. The three of us could be cozy in the loft, make a fire and stay warm, together.

Jaxon pulls a loaf of bread from the cupboard and then opens the fridge. He grabs a bunch of sandwich fixings and sets them on the counter. Taking a knife from the drawer, he starts putting a sandwich together. I watch him, not wanting to be bossy, but I can't help myself.

"Let me do that," I tell him. "I can make these."

"Like hell are you making my sandwich."

"Well, I'm the woman. I can make it. And besides, I can't eat that," I say, pointing to the slices of bread slathered in yellow. "I hate mustard."

Jax laughs. "Really? You're gonna come in my kitchen and tell me I'm doing it wrong?"

"Mustard is just gross."

"Honey, take a seat. I'll make you your sandwich, and I promise you'll like it."

I shrug, knowing I'm not going to get anywhere with him. Pulling out a chair at the table built for two, I sit and watch him in the kitchen. It's interesting, I mean, I can't ever remember seeing my own father making something as simple as a peanut butter and jelly sandwich—let alone this ham and Swiss, lettuce and tomato masterpiece Jaxon is putting together.

My father always had someone serving him. It was always my mother or me, or now my younger sisters, waiting on him hand and foot. He was the head of the household; we needed to serve him.

But it doesn't seem like Jaxon uses the same logic. He puts the ham sandwich on a plate, fishes a pickle out of a jar, and adds it to the lunch, and then hands me the meal.

I smile but, inwardly, fear rumbles though me. Maybe he won't see this baby as his responsibility. Maybe he won't want, or even offer, to take care of it.

What will I do then? I can't have this baby at home, without a husband. But looking at Jaxon now, seeing the scrawling tattoos across his skin and the beer he carries to the table, hearing the coarse words that fall from his lips, it might be a stretch to think a baby would cause him to become a father.

"So you back with that asshole?" he asks.

The sandwich is near my mouth and, even though it's full of mustard, I have to admit that it's way more appealing than anything Subway has ever made me. I pause, though, before I take a bite.

"Back with who?"

"That asshole who showed up here and yanked you back to your cult?"

"Oh, Luke? No, we aren't together. He's actually long gone. Went to Colorado for Bible College. He and I are over. I mean, I think he would have considered me, for a second, but not once he found us …."

"Naked?"

"Right." Heat rises to my cheeks, so I fill in the intensity of Jax's single word by shoving the sandwich in my mouth.

"So what did your parents do?" he asks.

"Oh, they don't know about the baby."

"No," Jax shakes his head. "About you. You left here all terrified that they were gonna kick you to the curb because you got properly fucked. Did they?"

"I'm still living at home." I pick up the dill pickle and take a crunchy bite. Smiling, I add, "They did send me to a sex addicts meeting though."

"You shitting me?" Jax takes a swig of his beer, cocking a brow at me.

"I know, and they only thought I had sex once." I laugh, grateful that Jax has pulled me from the stress of what happens next, and instead helped me remember to laugh. "Who knows what would have happened if they knew the truth—that after Luke showed up, we went for another round."

"You ready for another round now?" Jax asks as I take another huge bite from the sandwich.

Swallowing, I say, "Sure." At this point I just want to avoid the potentially awkward and traumatizing conversation that we have to have eventually. For now, ignorance is bliss.

"The mustard isn't bad, right?" Jax asks, as I stand from the table.

"Yeah," I say. "I guess I don't always know what is good for me."

"Well, honey, I have one thing that will always be good for you." Jax takes me by the waist and pulls me to him.

I lean in, realizing I want anything he offers up.

CHAPTER THIRTEEN

JAX

I HAVE this honey stripped of her clothes in five seconds flat. I know we just fucked in the woods, but I swear to God, watching her mouth on that dill pickle got me hard as a fucking log. I needed her lips wrapped around my cock the same way. And I won't wait.

Luckily, Harper has spent her whole life being repressed, and she must view the woods as the only place she can let loose. Watching her rip out of her clothing tells me everything I need to know. This girl is ready to have her mind blown.

I take off my pants, my cock standing at attention, the long, thick rod already throbbing, just imagining her mouth sucking me off nice and good. I want this girl on her knees, and I want to watch as she takes me in her mouth until my cock hits the back of her throat.

I watch Harper fling her bra to the floor. Her big, gorgeous tits now free, she teases me by taking her hand and rubbing it over her milky globe. She licks a finger, pinches her own nipples, then dips it low, between her legs, and presses her delicate finger into herself.

"Jax, I know I said your cock was pretty before—but it's really, really gorgeous. Like, when you undress, and I see how big and hard you are, it makes me want to do things ... things that I don't even know if we *can* do."

"Things like what, honey?" I ask, walking toward her. Knowing nothing is off limits. Feeling the heat rise in Harper, it rises in me too.

"Things like you coming on my face. On my tits." Harper's breathing is heavy as she speaks so erotically. Her finger is still pressed inside her, moving faster and faster, and she tells me her fantasies. "Things like you pushing my face into a pillow and coming in me from behind, and spilling your seed on my ass. Things like you and me in a shower, together, and me putting your cock in my mouth as hot water falls around us, as I swallow your come."

I love that Harper isn't embarrassed, isn't

ashamed. So many women probably Google this shit, find novels to read about these forbidden desires, but aren't brave enough to ask for it. I feel like a fucking king to have Harper standing before me, fingering herself as drops of her own pussy juice slide down her leg, telling me about the fact she wants me to give her a motherfucking facial. I'll come all over her gorgeous body, she doesn't have to ask twice.

"We can do all those things, baby." I slap my hand across her ass, and a sly smile spreads across her face.

"All of it?"

"Well, one thing at a time." I laugh, slapping her ass again. She moans in pleasure, and I squeeze her soft cheeks.

"What first?" she asks.

"You sure you don't want to pick?"

"I like it when you tell me what to do," she says, her eyes looking toward the ground.

I use a finger to draw her face back to mine. "Don't look away when you talk to me. I can dominate you in this cabin, when we have sex—but I'm not some asshole like the men you grew up with. I like to fuck, sure, but I don't see women as property, as things I can own. You are your own goddamned person. Got it, Harper?"

"Yeah," she says quietly. "Got it."

"Good. Then get on your knees and start sucking my cock."

She does as she is told. She kneels before me and takes the hair tie from her wrist and secures it around her long blond locks. Her face is exposed and, on her knees before me, she looks as if she's worshipping the fucking sex-god that is my cock. She dips her head forward and begins to suck my rod.

She moans as she takes me in her throat. I love the way her perfect tits move as she goes up and down. Her mouth is so warm around my cock, and I feel my veiny hardness mounting in pleasure. I feel the tip of my cock hit the back of her throat and I know she likes it rough by the way she takes me deeper and deeper.

One hand holds my ass, and the other fondles my balls as she sucks hard. She pulls my cock out of her mouth, and begins softly sucking on one ball, then the next, rubbing my shaft with her hand as she does. She is slurping on me as she sucks, and I can tell she's really getting into it when she puts my length back in her mouth and moves a hand down to her pussy. She starts rubbing nice and hard, her moans intensifying.

"Oh, Jax, oh, oh, oh," she screams, as her body quakes, her back arches as both her fingers move to her pussy. One hand is buried deep in her folds and the other is at the top, rubbing in circles as she gets herself off.

I love watching her come; her orgasm is a fucking thing of beauty.

She is still on her knees and when her orgasm passes, doesn't hesitate, she pulls my thickness back in her mouth as my cock throbs, so good and ready.

"I'm gonna come all over your tits, Harper," I tell her.

She obeys, pulling me out of her mouth and tugging softly at me as I shoot my seed across her chest. She bites back another moan as she watches my milky come cover her soft skin.

When we're done, I go to the bathroom and get her a wet washrag. She smiles coyly as she cleans herself.

"So ... that was pretty wonderful," she says, suppressing a yawn, unsuccessfully. We're both undressed, and I really fucking wish I had a couch right about now, so we could sit down and I could just play with her pussy while she takes a cat nap.

"Wanna lie down upstairs?" I ask. "You look tired."

"Sure. But then we need to talk, right?"

"Hey, honey, this afternoon delight was your idea as much as mine. We don't have to sleep.

We can talk right now if you want. I don't really give a fuck."

And I don't. Not because I'm an asshole, but because during the last few months out here all alone I've come to understand a few things. Mainly: whatever will be will be. I'm not about to get all strung out over a woman getting pregnant. Worse things can happen.

Harper seems relieved because her shoulders droop and she lets out a deep sigh. "Let's not talk yet. Let's take a nap."

So I smack her ass softly, and lead her to the loft.

HARPER

When I wake up from the nap, I see that Jax is sitting up in bed, reading something in a leather-bound notebook.

"Hey," I say, noticing the sun has begun to set. "What time is it?" I keep the blanket wrapped around my body, still naked from this afternoon.

"After five."

"Oh, wow. I need to be home tonight."

"How long's the drive to your parents' place?"

"About three hours," I tell him, swallowing back my nerves. I let myself stay in a sex-bubble all afternoon, but I can't stay there forever. Eventually it is bound to pop. I need to talk this out with Jaxon. "So, I'm pregnant, Jaxon. And I don't know what we should do."

"What do you wanna do?" he asks me, setting down his notebook. "You're the woman; it's your body. You're the boss."

"Yeah, but it's your baby," I tell him, confused. Sure, I'm carrying this child, but it's just as much Jaxon's as it is mine. I notice him cringing slightly. "What? I mean, I'm really sorry to come here and tell you that you're going to be a father, but it was God's—"

"If you say this was God's will, I'm gonna have to punch a hole in something. You're pregnant, Harper, not carrying Jesus-fucking-Christ."

"Well, okay," I say, feeling flustered. "But still, I get that me coming here and telling you this is shocking ... but I can't do this alone."

"You don't have to do this alone," he tells me, reaching for my hand.

Relief washes over me. "Oh, I'm so glad to hear you say that. I thought I might have to raise this baby by myself and—"

Jax cuts me off again. "Wait, you're keeping it?"

"What do you mean?" I ask.

"I mean, I get it, Harper—accidents happen

and we never used a single fucking condom. But it's not the end of the world. I mean, there is no way you could have this baby, you live at home. Your parents would literally kill you. And you have no life skills. I mean, honey, you're fucking amazing in bed, but how would you support a human?"

I pull my hand away, horrified at Jax's words. "Wait, you think I should have an abortion?"

"Well," Jax shrugs. "I don't know what you should do. I mean, you should do what you want to do—I just wonder how you think you'll be able to do this on your own."

"You said I didn't have to be alone." My words are filled with shock, with complete and utter disappointment.

"That's when I thought you wanted to go to a clinic. I wouldn't make you do that by yourself." Jax throws his hands up, frustrated. "Look, I'm not being an ass. I'm a realist."

"Well, I'm this baby's mother. And I don't know, Jaxon, I thought you'd step up to the plate, be a man. Not send me to the curb." I stand and move for the ladder. I need to leave, now. I need to be somewhere safe, somewhere that I don't even know exists.

"Harper, don't go like this." He scrambles down the ladder after me. "If you want this baby, of course I'll help. I'm not some deadbeat.

I'm just surprised, is all. You seem like the kind of girl who wants to wear white on her wedding and make babies with some God-fearing man. Not me. So, yeah, I'm a little surprised you wanna go through with this. An abortion might make more sense is all. So then later, when you have the husband and the picket fence, you can make a baby with someone you actually love."

Tears fall down my cheeks as I dress myself. I can't believe I let myself fantasize about living here in this cabin with Jax. He wants me to get rid of our baby. He's not the man I thought he was. Not the man I can be with.

I thought he would know how much being a mother means to me. It's all I've ever wanted. I watched my mother have nine children, and I witnessed the births of each one. I grew up knowing this was my calling, my destiny.

Of course this is going to be hard, a struggle. Of course this is not the dream I had for myself. But dreams change. The moment I saw a positive line on that pregnancy test, I knew that this baby was mine.

"I know I asked for your help, Jaxon, but I changed my mind. I can't have your help if you even for a second considered not raising this child with me. I can't be with a man like that." I pull open the front door, just needing to leave.

"You're being insane. Like, literally insane,

Harper," he says, coming after me. "I'm not the one running. I'm not kicking anyone to any curb. Fuck, I don't even have a curb. I have a dirt road. Stay on this dirt road. Stay and figure this out."

I open my car door, but before I slide in I call out to him, "I can't stay with a man like you. Let me go and figure this out on my own. If I ever need anything, I'll get in touch with you. But Jaxon, I won't need your help. I won't need you for this. I may be a woman without much life experience, but I will make up for it in love. I will be a good mother."

I turn the ignition, grateful that the snow is long gone and that the road is clear.

I just wish I were going on an easier path.

CHAPTER FOURTEEN

JAX

After Harper leaves I chop down mother fucking trees for days. I don't know what happened, but some animalistic insanity is going on up here in the woods. Screw those guys who are in Spartan races and shit. Give me an axe and a tree, and I'll cut anything to the ground.

The whole time, I'm yelling at myself for being a fucking idiot. Telling a woman—a woman like Harper—that I'd go to a clinic with her? Was I just trying to be the biggest dick-wad ever to live?

Buck shows up a week later. My beard is getting mangy, and fuck showers. I'm a man living in the woods. I don't need shit like soap.

Buck disagrees.

"Dude, you're freaking me out."

"What the hell do you care?" I ask, handing him a beer. We sit on stumps in the tree-graveyard I've created.

"Well, here's the thing, you seem cool and all," Buck starts, "but bro, you're a little off your rocker. You have a plan with all this wood?"

I look around my growing piles, the heaps of timber that could sell for a pretty penny.

"What the fuck do you care?"

"You sure you're good?" Buck takes a sip of beer and looks off in the distance. He doesn't seem to want to meet my eyes.

"What the fuck is this, some sort of one-man intervention?"

"Well, do you know anyone else around here? I mean, shit, I've Googled you, Jax. Saw you were part owner in a trucking company at one point. I don't know, but people in town are talking. They think you're some crazy man living in a piece of shit cabin—that you might be ...."

"Might be what?"

"Might be certifiable."

"I'm not crazy," I tell him.

"That's what every crazy person says."

"It's complicated." I shake my head.

"I thought you said you moved out here to avoid complications?" Buck cocks his head, rightfully questioning me.

"Look, you wanna know the truth of why I decided to fuck my life back home? I screwed the Sheriff's daughter. He got pissed. She was barely legal, but it was pretty damn clear she'd been around the block. Still, the Sheriff pinned his daughter's issues on me.

"I had a reputation—a big one, sure—but fuck, that girl did too. Her father screwed with our business. I cared too much about what my partner Dean and I had built. So I skipped town. It's for the best."

Buck nods. "Okay, well, that sucks. You were some man-whore and it bit you in the ass. But explain why you've been up here chopping wood all week like a goddamned lunatic?"

"I've been chopping wood since I moved out here."

"Not like this. Not until your hands bleed and you look like a wild bear."

"It doesn't matter," I tell him, finishing my beer, finished with this conversation, too.

"Get cleaned up and come into town tonight."

"Why you always trying to get me to come out with you?"

Buck laughs. "Uh, because I have no game. But last time I went out with you, I actually got laid. I'd like to repeat that."

I feel bad for the bastard. I've never had trouble finding pussy, so I can't relate. But I can sympathize. Wanting something and not being able to have it fucking blows.

God. All I've been thinking about is Harper. Her sad, pale blue eyes. The way she ran from my cabin, just like that family of deer ran from us in the woods. She got scared and scampered off. And now all I want is her back.

"Fine, fuck it." I shrug. "I'll meet you tonight. Seven good?"

"You'll shower first?"

I brush Buck off, and head into my cabin.

"See you tonight, dumbass," he calls as I shut the door.

I'll go out, make sure everyone knows I'm not some fucking lunatic. And try to figure out what the fuck I'm gonna do to get Harper back so we can at least talk. Make a plan. One that will keep her from running away.

HARPER

I drive home without stopping. I know when I arrive at my parents' place I'm going to be in trouble. I lied and stayed out so late. They won't know about the sex, but I bet they'll know something doesn't add up.

And the thing is, I can't handle any more judgment from them. I wish I had a girlfriend I could talk to about all this, but all my church friends are already married, with one or two babies cradled in their arms. They won't understand the sinful choices I've made. The choices I want to keep making.

The choices I can't make because Jaxon isn't a good, honorable man. We don't share the same values—so how could we raise a child together?

Not that he offered to marry me and sweep me away from my parent's condemnation. Of course he didn't; he'd never want to be with someone like me. He makes jokes about God and morality every chance he gets. He doesn't understand my value system.

But right now I don't really understand my value system, either. It's a system that has shunned me for weeks. That makes me keep secrets and hide in shame. It's a rigid system that binds me up in a box. I want to run free.

And I hate that I'm not like my church friends. Girls who grew into women who became wives, wearing chastity rings, who saved their bodies for their marriage beds.

When I pull up to the house, I offer up a small prayer to a God who seems to have abandoned me. *Please let them be gracious when I tell them I'm with child.* I have to tell them. There's no way I can do this pregnancy on my own.

I enter the quiet house—it's after eight at night, and my siblings are all in bed. Mother and Father sit in recliners, shaking their heads at me when I enter the room.

"Harper, where have you been?" my father asks, standing as I walk toward him.

"I went to...." I pause. Should I tell them the truth? If I don't, what does that say about my faith? My family? I need to give them a chance to accept me. "I went back to the cabin to see Jaxon."

My father slaps me across the face. I shriek, pull away, and grab my cheek in horror.

He's done this before, of course—when I was younger, when I disobeyed and neglected my chores, my household duties. When I read in bed when I should have been helping my mother. When I didn't memorize bible verses, or fell asleep during the six-hour church service. But never since I've become a grown woman.

My mother drops her head in shame. Shame of me, not my father.

"Harper how dare you defile your body and then come in my house."

"I didn't—" I stop talking. What would I say? I don't want to be a liar. I don't. And I don't want to say anything that could anger my parents further. I have a child growing within me; I need to be safe, healthy.

I need a plan.

CHAPTER FIFTEEN

JAX

IT'S BEEN over a month since Harper stormed away, and I finally figured out a way to fix things with her, a way to apologize for being a jackass, but I think it might be worse for my mental state. Because now I'm obsessed with her, with everything Harper. With her curves and her smile and her soft, generous words.

I need to go to the city and knock on every door until I find her—but not until I finish this project. Not until I can make it up to her. I'll finish today or tomorrow, then I can make a plan to find her.

When I'm in town getting my packages at the post office, checking email, and proving to

Buck that I'm not some creep in the woods, I decide to call Dean.

Talking things out with him has always been my mode of operation, and maybe he can help me figure out my next steps with Harper. I know Buck offered to let me confide in him, but that boy is over his head with women as it is—no way is he gonna be able to give me advice.

And Dean is one of those blue-collar, salt-of-the-Earth good guys. He is my fucking polar opposite, and that's why we've always gotten along.

He picks up right away. Not a dick like me, who screens calls and puts shit off.

"Everything okay?" he asks.

"Not exactly. Things have gotten complicated out here," I admit. But how do I tell my oldest friend that I got a girl pregnant, when my dealings with women is the very reason I fucked up my part of the business? The reason I left him to handle the hauling company on his own.

"Wanna talk?"

"Yeah, but not here," I say, looking around the crowded general store. "Shit, I'm at the post office. I don't have service at my cabin."

"I'll come out there tomorrow," he offers. See, he's good guy. I didn't even have to ask.

"Thanks, man."

"Hey," he says. "You see last month's deposit?"

"Yeah, what have you been doing?" I ask. "Working with the mob? That kind of money is what we were hoping to see in six years, not two."

"I know, right?"

I can't help but think I'm what held our business back. Me. Once I was gone, it started to thrive. I was the fucking problem.

"Don't go there, Jax," Dean says. "I know what you're thinking."

"Do you?"

"Yeah," Dean snorts. "I've known you since we were kids, and you've always had a complex. Always thinking you were the problem when things went south. It's just a coincidence that D & J Hauling found some success once you left."

"Okay, Dean," I say shortly. "Thanks for clearing that up."

"Don't be an ass. I'll see you tomorrow. Late afternoon."

I hang up, and head home. I have work to do.

HARPER

After my father slaps me, I retreat. I try to go back to before, before Jaxon, before Luke left. I try to go back to being the girl my parents require of me.

It mostly feels impossible.

So with each week that passes, I feel small in ways I never thought I could be.

I'm past the first trimester of this pregnancy —and it's getting near impossible to hide it. I remember my mother staying quite small throughout the nine months, but I feel so large already.

I put on the loosest clothing I can find and hope it conceals things. Thankfully the morning sickness has faded, but the fear in my chest is still here, pressing in on me with each step I take. With each dish I wash, with each math problem I help my younger siblings solve, with each lie I tell myself.

Lies about why I'm here ... lies about why I left Jaxon ... lies about how I am going to do this by myself when I don't even have my own checking account ... lies about how long I'm going to be able to hide this from my family. Eventually they're going to find out I'm having a baby.

But I can't face that now. Not yet.

I'm hollow in a way I've never been before. Like, I keep trying to hold myself together, but the more this secret weighs down on me, the more shame I feel. It's a vicious cycle. I need someone to confide in.

So I make a call to the clinic—the clinic that offers free support. The clinic I never thought I would need to enter, but I do. It breaks my heart because I always thought the church would be the place I would turn to when times were hard.

But the place my father runs is not a safe haven, not now. Maybe it never was. I press my hand to the cheek he slapped, wondering when his hitting me became love? How does his slap across my face equal care?

And I don't know how to be brave, be honest. Because the thing I need to tell my father—the thing I am still trying to hide—is going to change his shallow view of me into something nonexistent.

I'm not ready to lose my family, not when I have nothing to replace them with.

"I'm headed to Jana's house now," I tell my mother. We're standing in the kitchen. Breakfast dishes are cleared away, and my siblings are set up on their schoolwork in the basement. I've planned my appointment this morning with precision.

A big baking day is planned at Jana's house for most of the day. She's a member of our congregation and about my age. We grew up together. Of course she's married now, with a ten-month-old little girl.

When I told my parents I planned on attending, they were actually glad. I've avoided church activities as much as possible, but they keep encouraging me to make my way back into the fold. I figure I'll go to the appointment, then head over to Jana's, and no one will realize I'm an hour late.

"Alright, Harper," Mom says, her voice as meek as ever. "Drive safe."

Her long braid is over her shoulder, and I am hit with how young she is. She had me when she was eighteen years old; she married my father ten months before I was born. She's not even forty, and it shows. Her face is as fresh and young as ever. I wonder if she regrets giving her life away before she even knew what it was to be a woman?

On impulse, I wrap my arms around her and give her a hug. We aren't affectionate in general, and it's been worse since the night at Jaxon's, but part of me wants my relationship with her restored. I know I'll need her help, once I have my child.

"I love you, Mom," I say, kissing her cheek.

The clinic isn't cold or sterile at all. There are couches in the waiting room, and the receptionist smiles brightly. I don't know what I expected. Something harsh. Fluorescent lights, or a curt woman at the front desk.

I take the clipboard she hands me and sit with my legs crossed, trying to fill it out as vaguely as possible. I go so far as to lie about my last name. I write *Harper Free* in the blank space, instead of my actual last name, Baker.

Age: 21

Weight: I don't even want to know .... Literally nothing can button over my waist.

Medical history: n/a

I don't add that my siblings and I never had vaccinations, that we never had a pediatrician. That birth control is against our beliefs. I don't mention the fact that I don't take prescriptions or Tylenol because I've been taught to believe that God will cure my ailments, and if I'm sick it's because I am in sin.

I don't say any of that. Not here, not on this sheet of paper.

Instead, I wait in silence.

"Harper?" A nurse calls me back, and I follow her down the corridor. She takes my weight ... okay, not too insane. Still, I've gained sixteen pounds, which seems high. She takes my blood pressure, has me pee in a cup.

I do what she asks, then she gives me a gown and directs me to my room.

I change quickly, sit on the paper-lined examination bed. A few minutes later, there's a light tap on the door, and a woman doctor steps in.

"Hello, Harper, I'm Doctor Vance."

"Hi," I say nervously.

"So, I understand you're pregnant, but haven't seen any care provider yet?"

"Not yet. I don't really have a doctor, and I can't tell my parents ... so I don't know."

She nods, then flips through the file she brought in with her.

"You are twenty-one though, correct?" she asks.

"I am. I just, I live at home and don't really have a means to support myself ... exactly."

"But you intend to carry this pregnancy to term?"

"I do."

"Okay, Harper, here's what we'll do. After we perform an ultrasound, we can determine the due date, and then I am going to have you make an appointment with one of our counselors on site. They're experienced helping women in situations like yours make a plan that is most sustainable for both you and the baby."

"Okay." I nod, blinking back tears. I don't

know what I was hoping for. Her to become my confidante or something? Which is unrealistic; I get that. I just can't wait for another appointment to tell someone how stressed out I am. If my parents kick me out, where will I go? I have no support beyond my church family. And how much longer can I hide this pregnancy? I've already outgrown every piece of clothing I own.

Doctor Vance has me lie back, and a nurse comes in with an ultrasound machine.

She puts cool gel on my tummy and asks me to confirm the date of conception.

There is absolutely zero doubt in my mind when that occurred, so I answer with confidence.

Soon there is at the soft pitter-patter of a heartbeat.

But then Doctor Vance pauses. Tilts her head.

"Oh, Harper," she says in shock, looking at the screen, transfixed by the image before us.

"Oh, my God," I say, not at all taking the Lord's name in vain.

This cannot be happening. Not to me.

CHAPTER SIXTEEN

JAX

I SPENT all morning putting the finishing touches on my apology. Hopefully Dean will have some ideas of how I can go about finding the elusive Harper. Without knowing her last name, finding her might be difficult.

But I have to make things right with her. Especially since I'm confident she's planning on carrying the baby to term. The look on her face when she left confirmed everything I needed to know. Harper wants this child.

But, shit, finding her isn't gonna be easy. I don't know about knocking on the door of every church asking each preacher if they have a daughter with perfect tits and a perfect ass, who's carrying my baby.

Probably wouldn't go over too well.

I'm getting out of the shower when I hear a car pull up in my driveway. Huh, I didn't think Dean would be here for several hours. It's barely noon. I wrap a towel around my waist and look through a window.

My jaw drops—and I know, that's a pretty lame girl-move right there. I'm a grown ass man, I shouldn't be surprised by much. But I swear, seeing that hatchback come to a stop at my front door surprises me like a motherfucker.

Harper has returned.

I immediately regret the fact that I didn't come to her. Fuck. I should have found her.

But here she is, getting out of the car, coming to me first.

And I'd be a liar if I said my cock wasn't growing at the sight of her. She's curvier than ever. Under all those layers she's wearing, I see the gorgeous rise of her chest, the fullness in her cheeks. I'm more than glad. Last time she was here, she looked like a hollowed-out shell. Now she looks more like the woman I met three months ago.

I'm standing here in my towel, but I don't give a shit. I need to make things right with Harper. I need to apologize and I can't wait for pants and a shirt, shoes and socks. I already feel like such a fucking dick.

"Harper," I say, my voice solemn. "I'm so glad you came back."

"Oh, Jaxon," she says. Her slight smile erases my fear that she'll reject my apology. "Jaxon, I'm so sorry." She runs into my arms, and I pull her into an embrace.

"I didn't think I'd be seeing you here," I tell her, kissing the top of her head as I hold her tight. "And shit, honey, what the hell are you apologizing for?"

"I shouldn't have left. I'm still upset about that day I ran out ... but the truth is, I can't do this alone. And now I know that more than ever."

"What do you mean?" I ask, pulling away slightly so I can look in her eyes. They are pools of crystal clear water. Water I need. "What happened?"

"It's too much, Jaxon. I can't even believe it." She falls against my chest and begins to cry. I know pregnant women are extra emotional but, damn, every time I see Harper she's a puddle.

"Hey, hey, don't cry, baby." Shushing her, I take her hand and lead her inside the cabin. "Sit down, catch your breath. And let me take care of you."

I guide her to the leatherback rocker by the fireplace, and even though it's a nice spring day, I throw some logs on. A fire always relaxes people. And Harper looks chilled to the bone with whatever has gone on.

I pull on my jeans in the bathroom and then, walking over to the kitchen, I put on the teakettle. Women like tea when they're upset, right?

She's sniffling in the chair, her shoulders heaving. The whistle on the kettle blows and I put a bag of chamomile in the mug. While it steeps, I pull out a bottle of whisky and pour myself a solid double. My dog Jameson is at my feet, and I pat his butt, telling him to go sit with Harper. He obeys and I watch her sigh as his heavy frame curls up at her feet.

"Listen," I tell her, handing her the mug. I sit in the chair opposite her, my liquid courage in hand. "I have to tell you something."

"No," Harper interrupts, wiping tears from her cheeks. "Let me go first. Let me tell you why I came here today. Why I had to come."

"Harper, I've just gotta talk for a second, alright? Besides, you're still crying. I can't handle you talking when you're also sobbing. It's too damn heartbreaking."

That gets a small laugh from her, and she stifles a cry with her hand. "Okay, Jaxon, go ahead then."

"Harper, there is hardly anything I know about you besides the fact your body is heavenly.

Your words are pure. Your curiosity gets me fucking hard."

I cough, trying to gather my thoughts. I thought I'd have more time to prepare the perfect speech, but fuck, when do things go as planned?

I keep going, "I mean, what else do I know? You have a fucked-up family." When she winces at that, I try again, "You have a family that's a lot different than me. And honestly, I think they are a lot different than you, too. But besides those things, I don't know your favorite food or color or movie or song.

"And so when you came here, telling me you were having my kid and wanted to do this whole thing—raise it—together? Shit, girl, I didn't say the right things to you, the things you needed to hear—because, Harper, I've never been with a woman like you. A woman who needs the things you need. But, honey, I will give you that. I will try."

"Jaxon," she says shaking her head. "You don't need to come on a white stallion and save me. I'm not asking you to change everything and be my ... whatever. I just couldn't believe the person I got pregnant with would ask me to not be a mother. Being a mother is the only thing I've ever wanted."

"Okay, but Harper, I don't know that. I

didn't know that. So I wasn't trying to offend you by suggesting options. I was trying to be chivalrous. I was trying to let you know there was no right or wrong way to move forward."

"I shouldn't have left angry. It wasn't right of me. How could I expect you to know that being a mom is my dream?"

"Harper, I don't know shit. I don't even know your last name."

"Baker. Harper Baker."

I nod. "I'm Jaxon Lane."

"Nice to meet you, Mr. Lane," Harper says, setting down her tea on the side table. Good, I think the tears have finally stopped.

"Harper, I really am sorry."

"Thank you," she says. "For the apology. For letting me in here."

"Harper, shit, of course I'd let you in."

"How would I know, Jaxon? It's pretty clear you have a history with women. How was I to know there wouldn't be one with you today?"

"How do you know my history?"

"You seem to know what you're doing is all," Harper says. "I mean, with me." She lowers her eyes, blushing. "When I'm undressed."

I smile, shaking my head. "Well, listen, I haven't had a woman up here, not once. That's not why I came to the woods."

"Why did you come here?" she asks.

"Because I needed to breathe."

That makes Harper start crying again, and fuck me now. "What did I do now?"

"I just. You came here to breathe and I've just made everything a million times more complicated."

"Not a million times more complicated. Just one time more complicated," I tell her, smiling, pointing to her stomach.

She doesn't respond, she looks so undone.

I don't ask her any more questions because, while I may not know much about Harper, I do know one thing she likes. One thing she likes a hell of a lot.

Standing, I walk toward her and pull her up.

Without speaking, I take off her jacket, her sweater. After pulling off her tank top, taking in her gorgeous breasts, just fucking full and larger than ever, I get on my knees and tug off her boots, her socks, her leggings. I slide my hands over her bare thighs, resting my fingers at the waistband of her panties. I tease her, just grazing my thumb over them.

Then, noticing her swollen abdomen, I swallow hard, realizing that she really is having my child. Harper is going to birth my offspring.

It's not that I didn't know this in theory—of course I did. And yeah, I never expected to be a father so soon. But it still seemed so far away when I was here alone in this cabin, thinking about it.

But I'm not alone right now.

Right now, I'm holding Harper in my arms, and our child is between us, and fuck, that is some heavy shit. Some fucking amazing shit. Shit that makes me hard in a way I never imagined.

My cock grows as I press my face, ever so slightly, to her stomach. She takes a sharp intake of breath at this movement, and I know she is taken by this moment too.

Then, as the desire mounts, I press my mouth against her covered pussy, breathing in the scent of her. Inhaling her, I kiss her, running my hand between her thighs, spreading her legs. I just want to be a man that makes Harper happy.

As I pull down her panties, the ones that are wet with her heat, I know I can make her happy in this moment, at the very least.

HARPER

Oh, my heart. I try to hold back, to not give in, because I know there are things I need to tell Jaxon. Soon.

But as his tongue slips into my opening, I forget everything I need to say. I forget everything because ... oh, that feels good. It feels so right.

His tongue darts into my folds. Each kiss, each hot breath of air on me, forces my legs to quiver a bit more, to spread a bit wider. When he lifts one of my legs and throws it over his shoulder, and my hands move to his shoulders for balance, I just about faint.

Because suddenly his head is pressed between my legs, licking my opening, and I feel my wetness seep out.

"Oh, Harper, you taste so fucking good," he says, cupping my ass with his hands. He pulls me to the bearskin rug, and I lie on my back, legs spread apart as he instructed. "Relax, honey, let me eat you."

So I do, my eyes close and I feel Jaxon completely devour me. As he uses a finger to press into my opening, I moan, arching my back, remembering the sensation of a climax and knowing I am getting closer to it. "Oh, Jaxon," I pant, strumming my hands through his hair as he adds another finger to my opening. He rubs his thumb in circles, causing my entire body to writhe in pleasure.

"Oh, yeah," I moan, "Oh, yeah, yeah, yeah." My body shakes as he hits a spot deep inside me, over and over again. "I need you in me, Jaxon," I beg. "Now."

I mean it. All I want is to see his thick, gorgeous cock. And even though I want to taste his come as I take him in my mouth, my pussy is screaming with desire, much louder than my brain.

And so when he pulls off his jeans, revealing that massive rod that fucked me and got me pregnant—the massive rod that fills my opening so good, so nice and tight—I feel the wave of an orgasm wash over me, just remembering. Just seeing him.

"I need it in me now," I tell him. Jaxon doesn't pause. He leans over me and presses his cock inside me, just like I begged him to do. My hunger for him covers me, the same way his mouth covers my own. His tongue finds mine, and once entwined, I taste myself on him. It makes my pussy come hard and fast, and at the same time his long cock hits me deep inside, a spot I could never find myself if I tried for a year. If I tried forever. Because Jaxon's manhood fills me in a way that nothing else could—nothing else should.

All I want is this cock in my pussy, for the rest of my life.

And it isn't fair to want Jaxon, a man who in so many ways is a stranger, to be mine, but I do. And it isn't just because he took my virginity. Isn't just because he got me pregnant. It's also because he's a man that no one else can compete with.

He lives alone in the woods, chops wood, and is dirty in ways that make me blush. His muscled arms and chiseled abs, his biceps covered in ink and his long beard, tell me he's wild and untamed. Those are the things that make me want Jaxon. Completely.

But they are also the things that confirm Jaxon will never commit, never be a husband, never be the things I really need.

His hardest pulses through me, as the waves of orgasm continue to ripple through my body. He pulls a nipple into his mouth and the very touch sends tingles through my core. Every touch, every time we come together, all I can think is that I want more. More of him.

When we finish, he takes my hands and lifts me up.

"I need to show you something," he says. "It's my apology gift."

I take a blanket from the back of the chair, and wrap it around myself. Jaxon pulls his jeans back on, and then points to the corner where something is covered in a sheet.

"That's yours."

"A present for me?"

"Yeah," he says, shrugging. "I made it. For you. I mean, I know you decided to have this baby ... and I don't know how you want me to support you in all of this ... but whatever you need, I'm here for you."

He doesn't offer to marry me, or something old-fashioned, and I don't expect him to. That would be too much, too soon.

Especially since I have to tell him something that is about to change all of this.

"Go on," Jaxon says. "Look."

Smiling, I walk over to the corner and lift off the sheet.

What he made for me leaves me gasping.

"Jaxon ... I don't know what to say. It's so thoughtful." Jaxon has carved a beautiful wooden cradle with his bare hands. I press my hand to it, and it sways gently on its rockers. Beautiful cedar is perfectly pieced. "I didn't know you worked with wood other than—"

"Chopping it?" Jaxon smirks. "Yeah, well I grew up making furniture with my dad. Thought I'd go into business with him someday, but he wanted to retire, travel. So I said, fuck it, I'll go into business with my buddy Dean instead. We have a wood hauling company now. Anyways," Jaxon shrugs. "Either way, I work with wood. And so I thought this is the peace offering you deserve. The baby and you deserve."

"It's beautiful," I say, holding back tears. Just

barely. The words I really need to say hanging on my lips.

"Hope those are happy tears, then, Harp," he says, smiling. "So you think this will work for the baby?"

"Um. Sort of." I look up at him, my heart laced with so much emotion, it's filled to the brim.

"What do you mean, sort of?" he asks, not understanding.

"Well, we're going to need two more," I tell Jaxon. The father of my children. "Because, Jaxon, I'm pregnant with triplets."

CHAPTER SEVENTEEN

JAX

NO FUCKING WAY. Triplets?

"Is this some prank, Harper? Because I don't get the joke." My chest pounds at the words, because fuck. This is just way too much. Too soon.

Her hand runs across the smooth wood of the cradle I've carved for our baby. Singular. And now ... her eyes are filled with emotions, but I don't know this woman well enough to know which emotions they are.

"It's not a joke. I wouldn't joke about this." She walks over to her purse, sitting by the leatherback chair, and pulls out pictures. Crossing back to me at the cradle, she hands them over. "See for yourself. Three babies, Jaxon. It's pretty obvious."

I take a deep breath and hold up the photos. The ultrasound images are damn clear, just as she said. Three distinct babies. A technician has typed a 1, 2, and 3 over the heads as if it wasn't clear enough. Oh, it's clear all right. Crystal.

"Say something...." Harper says. "I mean, I've been thinking about it all day, ever since Doctor Vance dropped the bomb. I just need you to say something. Anything."

Being a father was on the periphery of my mind, I guess. But shit, I'm twenty-eight years old. Not ready to be tied down in the least ... and this one-night stand has gotten ridiculously out of control. *Triplets*? Fuck, I'm way over my head.

"Jaxon, what are you thinking?"

What the hell am I supposed to say to her? That I just wrapped my head around one kid, and now we're having three? That I'm trying to be a fucking man here, but have no desire to be a father? Can't say that. She's already a mess; my truth would just destroy her.

"So what happens next?" I ask.

She huffs. And I know this moment is wrought with intensity and I should be fucking spinning out of control right now, but damn, she is adorable when she gets worked up.

"What happens next?" She snorts, suddenly sounding more of a cynic than I would have believed possible. "Next I push three people from my body."

"Okay, I know that," I say, raising my hands in defeat. "I mean, like, what did the doctor say? Are the babies healthy? Are you healthy?"

Maybe I finally said the right thing, because at least she begins wiping her tears away.

"They're healthy. And I guess I'm not surprised about there being more than one baby in there, because I really am huge for only being three months along. I've seen my mother carry so many children, and she never showed like this, so soon. But it's pretty obvious I won't be able to hide it from them much longer."

"And you *want* to hide it?" I ask. Her family dynamics are seriously screwed up. It's one thing if she was sixteen year old–but Harper is a woman. She shouldn't be scared of her parents.

"I just know that as soon as I tell them ... my life will change. Forever."

"How so, exactly?

"They'll never look at me the same way. My place in the church family will change. Everyone will see me as less-than, used. Everyone will think I'm a sinner." Harper walks over to the chair by the fireplace and sits down with her hands on her stomach, protectively.

I sit in the chair beside her, looking for words that won't upset her—or at least for words that won't upset her more.

"But you said you wanted babies ... to be a mom. Do you still mean that, now that you're having triplets?"

"I don't know, Jaxon. When Doctor Vance pointed to the three beating hearts, it felt like ... I know this sounds weird, but it felt like a miracle. Like, for some reason I have the privilege of carrying three babies? That's amazing. But then, driving here, the weight of it started to overwhelm me. Like, I can barely stand on my own two feet, and now I'll have three pairs of feet depending on me ... for everything. I don't even have a home of my own, any means of supporting them—how can I expect to do this?"

"I'll help. I'll do whatever you need."

"What does that even mean, Jaxon?"

"I don't know," I tell her, honestly. Because I have no fucking clue what it means. I just know I need to step up to the plate. Somehow.

"I need more than *I don't know.*"

"Fuck, Harper, you can live here," I say, running my hands through my hair, throwing out the first thing that pops into my mind. "I have money, I'll give you money."

"Money isn't going to solve everything."

"In this situation, it'll solve an awful fucking lot."

I stand, a ball of nerves. Did I seriously just tell Harper she can move in? What the hell am I thinking? I go to the kitchen and pour a few inches of whiskey in a tumbler, then begin pacing the room.

"It just sounds ... crass," she says, her nose scrunched.

"Well, get used to it, honey. I'm a fucking man. Okay? I don't know what pansy-ass preachers boys you've spent your life with, but that ain't me."

"I know what you are, Jaxon. You are practically a stranger. And, no offense, you have an amazing body ... but I need more than that."

Now it's my turn to snort. "Beggars can't really be choosers, Harp."

"That isn't nice, to call me a beggar. I didn't mean to get pregnant."

"You're also the only woman I've ever met over the age of eighteen who isn't on birth control."

"I don't believe in using birth control, Jaxon. Which is just, like, the five hundredth thing you don't know about me."

I stop pacing, turn toward her. "Well, then, enlighten me, Harper, the mother of my children. Tell me what I need to know."

"You wanna know things about me, Jaxon?" She shakes her head, standing, and coming toward me. She stops at my feet, pointing her index finger at my chest. "Then you need to be nice and act like a gentleman and ask me questions about myself. Get to know me as someone other than a girl you like to sleep with."

"I'll do some of what you want, honey. I'll ask you questions and play nice, but I won't be a gentleman. I'm rough. And hard. I'm wild, and I think that is exactly why you're so undone when you're with me. You think you want to tame me, but you don't. A tamed man doesn't fuck like a free one."

Harper sucks in a sharp, quick breath, and I take that as my fucking cue. I wrap my arms around her and pull her into a deep, long kiss.

A kiss that keeps her from talking back, because, right now, I want her to remember why she returned. Why she's come back for me, come back for more.

She didn't come back here—twice—because she wants to talk. She keeps coming back because she wants to lose her fucking mind.

HARPER

His mouth on mine causes a stirring deep within me. Again. I swear this will never get old.

I love it when he tells me what I need, what I should want. I love it when he takes control ... because right now I am so over my head that I don't want to be in control at all.

Instead, I'll lose myself in him.

He says he'll let me stay here? Fine. I don't want to face reality at home.

He says he'll throw money at the situation? Good. Because I have literally zero dollars to pay for doctors and maternity clothes, and I'm not even thinking about the actual needs of infants. Times three.

He wants to kiss me, undress me, drop to his knees and lick me? Wonderful. Because, when he does that, he makes me forget.

Everything about his plan is better than the alternative, which is me going home and facing my family and figuring out how to be a grown-up. I don't want to grow up if it means less of Jax's mouth on mine. I don't want to be an adult if it means no more midday orgasms. No more of th—

Ohmigod ... Jax has pressed his hands down the front of my pants and ... ohh....

"Jax, that feels so ... so ...."

"Shush, honey. You need to stop thinking. You need to forget." It's as if he's reading my mind.

I squeak out, "Okay," before kissing him

again. His lips are so soft, and the complete opposite of his rough beard. His mouth devours mine, his tongue caressing my own as he holds the back of my head with one hand. I moan, pressing my body against his.

His other hand touches my folds, his fingers deftly finding the spot that turns my desire on in a deep, more heated way. He dips his fingers into my opening, causing me to claw at the waistband of his jeans, wanting him undressed. Now.

"I like it when you get all excited," he purrs in my ear. His hot breath sends a shiver across my skin.

I can't suppress my smile, and I don't want to. I want to give in to this moment, because that is what this cabin, what being with Jaxon has always offered—an escape.

Maybe that makes me weak, or a potentially terrible parent—but right now, I'm going to take Jaxon's hard, chiseled body as the gift it is. A gift that's mine to unwrap.

I unbutton his jeans, push them down until they fall on the floor. He doesn't even have any boxers on; he had just stepped out of the shower when I arrived. His hands tug on my pants, and he shimmies them off me, removing them and my panties in one fell swoop.

As I step out of my clothes, I take in Jaxon

from head-to-toe. His piercing eyes and strong nose, his beard that I remember tickled me when his head was buried between my legs, and the taut muscles stretched across his shoulders. His abs are solid, covered in ink just like his biceps. Everything about him is a piece of rugged art, something forged from the land, and right now I feel like he was created just for me.

And then, my eyes reach his cock, and I feel the contractions of my pussy, how needy it becomes so quickly when I look at his solid wood. His perfect, huge cock is hard as a rock. It's large, and solid, the skin stretched tight, and his groin is so irresistible, I feel drawn to it, to him. I just want to press my body tight against his, to feel his shaft against my skin.

"You like that, don't you, looking at my cock?" Jaxon asks.

I nod, biting my lip, my nipples tingling under my shirt, beneath my bra. I want him to take it off me, but I also want his fingers back on my pussy, his hands to slap my ass. I want his mouth breathing hot air in my ears, whispering words that make my core tremble.

I want so much. Mostly, I want him. Without thinking, I reach down to my opening, and I dip two fingers into my entrance. I'm so wet, so ready for him. I pull out my fingers, teasingly, and pull Jaxon closer, pressing my fingers in his mouth so he can suck off my juice.

He moans as he sucks my fingers. Then in one swift motion, he rips my shirt off, pulling it over my head, his eyes greedily looking down at my tits. They're so big right now; I swear they've doubled in size since I became pregnant.

He reaches behind me, growling as he does, as if he's overcome with a predatory desire. He unclasps my bra and my breasts fall out, unencumbered and ready for him to suck and lick, ready for him to press his hard cock against them, to come across my skin like he's done before.

"I want you so bad," I moan.

Good," he says, pulling back my hair, twisting it in his hands, tugging on it so my chin lifts, so I am looking right at him. "Because I'm gonna fuck you right now."

He lifts one of my thighs, smacks my ass. Carries me to the kitchen table, sweeping off the salt and pepper shakers, the paper towel roll, a book. He pushes them away, and sets me down on the bare wooden surface.

With my legs apart, he draws closer to me, his hands cupping my face as he kisses me again, deeply. His tongue is against mine, and as they are interlocked the heat continues to rise within me.

One of his hands lowers, grazing my nipple, thumbing it, and rubbing in a circle. Then he bends down, lifting it to his mouth. He sucks my breast and it stimulates every inch of my skin. I am so wet, I literally feel myself soaking his table.

I lean back, my arms holding me up on the table, and I feel so vulnerable, splayed out like this for him, but Jaxon seems to love it. Seems to want it just as bad as I do.

"Are you ready for my cock?" he asks, taking hold of himself, and guiding it into my opening. "Because I'm gonna fuck you hard and fast."

"Do that, do it like that to me," I pant. "Hard. I want it hard, Jaxon."

He smiles at me, his cocky grin so completely gorgeous.

"Oh, I'll give it to you hard."

He pushes himself into me—it's tight going in—and the pressure builds as he throws one of my legs over his shoulder, plunging deeper into my entrance.

"Oh, Jaxon," I moan, tossing back my head as he thrusts into me.

"I'm not even halfway in your pretty little pussy," he says, raising his eyebrow as he continues to fill me with his rod.

"It won't fit."

"Oh, honey," he tells me. "It'll fit. It has before."

"But this position?" I gasp. "I don't think I can take it."

"You'll take it, and when you do you'll come like a fucking fountain," he says, pulling my ass closer to his cock, his hands pawing at my flesh, as if I'm his to devour.

I want him to take all of me, like a beast, like a bear. I want this wild man to fill me with his seed like he did before. He's so powerful he put three babies in me. I want anything his cock is offering up.

He keeps pounding me, and the walls of my pussy pound, too—more like throb. I'm pulsing in pleasure as he fills me so nice and deep, sawing in and out, in and out, until every pressure point within me is on fire.

"Oh, Jaxon, it's so ... oh, God, it feels so good, so good," I moan, gripping his forearms as I climax. The orgasm ripples through me—a chill is sent over my skin, my entire body on fire and alive and hot and cold and everything. I feel everything. Everything good and pure and right.

And maybe I'm a hypocrite. Praying to God when I need him, and then taking his name in vain as Jaxon takes me, but oh, my heart, nothing feels as holy as Jaxon pressed deep inside me.

"Oh, yeah, oh, honey," Jaxon says, thrusting again. "Where do you want me to come?" he asks, as I pant for breath.

"Come in me, Jaxon," I beg. "Come in me now."

And he does. His warm seed fills me, and it is divine and it is like a prayer. Only better. Because my head isn't bowed. My eyes aren't closed. Right now, I am open, wide-eyed and alive.

CHAPTER EIGHTEEN

JAX

I HELP her off the table and she turns toward the bathroom. Looking at her walk away, I take in her silhouette. Her curvy hips and beautiful breasts are better than any woman's I've ever seen, but it's the slight bump on her stomach that seems to get me hard all over again.

Fuck, what is happening to me? It's like all of a sudden I'm not freaked out by the fact Harper is having my babies. I want her to have them. I want her to be filled with my flesh and blood. I want her to birth my son, my daughter. I mean, that fuck we just had was off the charts—but I can't believe I'm not running for the goddamned hills.

"Jaxon," she calls out. "Can you make more of that tea? It was delicious."

"Sure thing," I tell her. I pull on my jeans and grab a flannel off the back of a kitchen chair. Bending down, I pick up the things I tossed aside when I took her on the table. I can't help but smile over the way her pussy was splayed out there for me, just waiting to be fucked. She's so nice and tight, and thinking about it forces me to adjust myself in my pants.

Blowing the air from my cheeks, I try to cool it. Damn, Harper has me all fired up. Lighting the burner on the stove, I set the kettle back on. I like to fuck Harper, and the idea of her pregnant with my children makes me fucking horny as hell, but there is no way I can raise a fucking family.

Pouring myself a cold beer, I look around the tiny cabin I bought out here in the woods. It's on fifty acres, so there's plenty of space—but, shit, the loft barely holds my queen-sized mattress. There's no room in here for kids.

Let alone three of them. I take a sip, trying to figure out what that would even look like. I make enough off my share of the hauling company, but that set-up isn't going to provide for me forever ... and especially not for a herd of babies.

A knock on the door breaks my train of

thought, which is probably a good thing. I pull open the door, having totally forgotten Dean was coming over.

The timing wasn't perfect and, as Harper comes out of the bathroom—dressed, thank God—all I can think is that Dean is gonna take one look at the situation and think I haven't changed at all.

And, fuck, have I? First chance I had to be with Harper, I took it. And look where that got me. A hell of a lot more complicated than the Sheriff's daughter.

"Dean. Hey, man," I say, opening the door for him. I look between him and Harper as he steps inside. "This is Harper, she's my ... uh, she's Harper. And Harper, this is Dean, my business partner."

"And his oldest motherfucking friend," Dean says, slapping my back. "You gonna stand there or you gonna get me a beer?" he says to Harper.

Her eyes are innocent and full of surprise as she takes in Dean, who actually looks pretty damn similar to me. Beard. Tattoos. Flannel shirt. Boots. But she doesn't know he's a way nicer guy than me.

"Hey, sweetie, just teasing," he says to Harper, whose eyes have found their way to the floor. "I'd never ask you to do that. This asshole can get me a beer."

She raises her head as the kettle whistles. "It's no problem, Dean. I'm getting tea anyways." She scurries away, like a deer scampering in the woods, and I raise an eye at Dean.

"You gotta be nice to her," I say.

"You telling me how to treat a woman?" He sneers, good-naturedly. "Shit, Jax, I was just messing around."

"I know." I shrug, not even knowing where to begin with this. "It's just ... Harper is important."

I wanted to talk to him about Harper, about how to find her, and ask what he thought I should do next. But fuck, now he's here and she's here, and she's having triplets. I don't know where to begin.

"That's cool, just tell me what I need to know. What got so complicated you needed a motherfucking heart-to-heart?" he asks, laughing. He must see my blank expression, because he adds. "Shit, something happen for reals?" He looks over his shoulder at Harper, who's walking toward us with a frothy beer and a mug of tea.

"Here you go," she says, offering the beer to him. The beer is about three-fourths foam and I smile. She notices and shakes her head. "What?" she asks, pouting playfully. "I've never poured a beer. I didn't know how to do it."

"The girl Jax has in his cabin has never

poured a beer?" Dean clinks his glass with mine. "Now this I gotta hear."

"Not much to tell," I say. "Harper doesn't drink. Or swear. Or ... what else don't you do, Harp?"

"Truth is, Jaxon and I don't know one another very well, Dean," she says shrugging. "Maybe you could tell me more about your old friend?"

"What do you wanna know?" Dean walks over to the kitchen table, the same one where I just fucked Harper, and he takes a seat. Harper and I follow, and I see her cheeks redden as she grabs a paper towel and dabs at a spot on the table, still wet with her.

"Oh, just, like, who is Jaxon? Like, what sort of guy is he?"

Dean chuckles, setting down his glass. "Let's see. Jaxon never asks permission. He never gets a second opinion. And he certainly never asks for advice. Which is why it was so strange that my old friend called me, wanting to talk."

My jaw tenses and I instinctively look at Harper, trying to see how she absorbs Dean's assessment of me.

"Sounds about right, considering what I know about him," she says generously.

"And how *do* you know Jaxon, exactly?" Dean asks her.

"Well, funny thing—my car got stuck out here about three months ago, and Jaxon let me stay for the night. And then I visited about month ago, and then came back out today."

"Can't stay away huh?" Dean raises his eyebrows, clucking his tongue. "Aww, just teasing. That's good, Jax could probably use the company. You been out here for what, six months now?"

"About that," I say.

"So you have something on your mind?" Dean asks, putting me on the spot.

I look at Harper. Her hands are in her lap; she looks so small and out of place here with Dean and I.

"Go ahead, Jaxon," she says. "I'm sure that's why you wanted him to come out here."

I cough uncomfortably. Dean's a hard-ass in some ways, but he's a good, decent guy. He dates women and takes them out for dinner and a movie. He goes to his grandma's house for Sunday dinner. He is BBQs and Bud Light. He is apple pie.

I'm not a good guy like him. I'm the fucking a la mode.

And maybe it makes me a pussy, and I swear, it's not me I'm thinking about right now. I just don't want him to judge Harper for being with an ass like me.

"She's pregnant, Dean."

"Oh, shit," he says.

"With my triplets."

HARPER

Dean's sharp intake of breath has me in tears. Less than an hour ago I was on my back on this table, in complete denial. In complete escape mode. I pretended that Jaxon being inside me was enough. Enough for what?

Dean's panicked eyes tell me that this is actually real. Really happening. Triplets. Three human babies. Three babies that will require everything I have, and require things I don't even know yet. Things Jaxon and I—a complete bad boy and a completely sheltered girl—have no business learning, not together. Not now.

Not like this.

"Shit, guys, I'm sorry," Dean says, pulling his hand through his hair. "A one night stand turned into triplets? Fuck, that is like made-for-TV shit."

"That's not exactly helpful." Jaxon isn't laughing or joking anymore. His head has dropped, his shoulders heavy.

"I know." Dean looks at me warily. "Sweetie, you doing okay? Where do you live?"

"I live in Coeur d'Alene. With my parents."

Dean's eyes fill with panic. "You are legal, right?"

"I am." I try to speak calmly, because if I give in to the overwhelming thoughts running through my brain I'll fall apart. I need Dean and Jaxon to believe I'm a capable woman. Maybe if I convince them, I'll be able to convince myself next. "I'm twenty-one. And I know this is crazy ... but it will be okay. It's children, not zombies."

Dean lets out a controlled breath. "Jax, man, this is fucking nuts. What's the plan here? What do your parents think, Harper?"

"Well, it's still early. I'm only twelve weeks along. And, um ... I haven't exactly told them. Or anyone. I just found out myself."

Jaxon doesn't offer me his hand to hold, or a look of sympathy. I guess I shouldn't need it. Need him. But I do need him. I want him.

He surprises me when he looks up, nodding stoically. "She's gonna stay here for a while, Dean."

"Here?" Dean looks around the cabin. "You plan on keeping a pregnant woman, whose parents don't know what the hell is going on, in a cabin in the sticks, with no cell service. How in fuck's sake is that the responsible thing to do?"

I hear Dean, but I only have eyes for Jaxon. He meant what he said when he offered to let me stay. And a gust of relief blows over me. I needed his assurance that he wouldn't leave me out to dry, and he gave it.

"My next appointment isn't for a month. I don't need to see the doctor unless there is some sort of complication. So I can stay here." Going home felt impossible ... and now I don't need to.

"And what are your parents going to think?" Dean asks.

"What the hell does it matter? Harper is a grown woman. She can sleep in my fucking bed if she wants to, Dean."

"Dude, I don't care where she sleeps. But you called me, wanting my advice, and I'm giving it. You can't keep her here without telling her family. They'll think she was fucking kidnapped or some shit."

"I'm not calling them," I say, meaning it. There's no way I can pick up the phone and hear my father's berating tone when I tell him I'm with child. There's no way I can listen to him tell me why I'm immoral and a disgrace to the church. I can't and I won't.

"Harp," Jaxon says, grabbing my hand in an act of solidarity. I swallow; his hand on mine feels so warm. So right. "I think Dean's right in some ways. I don't want your father showing up here."

"Fine. I'll write him a letter. Let him know what's going on and that I'm safe."

"Okay," Jax says, nodding. "You do that. Dean can bring it back to town, right?" Jaxon looks over at his friend.

"That's fine." Dean's eyebrows are knit together, and his jaw is clenched; he's clearly not thinking any of this is fine. "Do you have clothes, things you need?" he asks me across the table.

"I don't have anything." I bite my lip, knowing that this is all so irresponsible, but also upset at my parents for setting me up this way. They kept me in such a tightly sealed box for my entire life, that I don't know how to be anything but helpless. I want to prove to Dean and Jaxon that I am self-sufficient ... even if I know I'm not. "But I can make clothing, all I need is some old fabric and a needle and thread. And I can make do on very little. And the doctor gave me prenatal vitamins before I left."

"You don't need to sew your own fucking clothes," Jaxon says, seemingly amused. A small smile is on his lips, and I can see how all he needs is a bit of a plan to feel like things are going to be okay. "I can go into town and order you some stuff. It will be here in a day."

"This is so fucking crazy." Dean finishes his beer, and stands for another. "Harper, while you write to your parents, Jax and I are going for a walk, okay?"

"Of course," I say. "And thank you ... for not judging us."

Dean laughs. "Oh, I'm judging you guys. I think you're both nuts."

Jaxon rolls his eyes and digs in a drawer for a pad of paper and a pen. Setting them before me, he grabs his beer and kisses my forehead.

"Be assertive," he tells me. "Don't beat around the bush. Tell them exactly what's up, what you think."

I watch as Jaxon and Dean leave the cabin, then I stare down at the blank page.

Tell them what I think? That is impossible in so many ways. Mostly because I don't really know what I think. Do I believe the teachings of my father's church? That what I'm doing with Jaxon is a sin? Am I unworthy because I let him inside me? Because I've also been taught to believe children are a gift, a blessing.

So isn't this actually a blessing times three? How can me being a mother be wrong, when I've been taught my entire life that it's the greatest calling by God for women? How can it be both ... how can I be a sinner and a saint?

I pick up the pen and try to put those thoughts into words that don't cast judgment on my parents ... but also bring those questions to light.

After I have written all of that I add a final paragraph.

I'm staying in the cabin with Jaxon for the time being. This choice is mine, as I'm a grown woman, a woman you have raised. In my heart, this is the right choice. You don't have to agree with my decision, and I understand you may condemn me, but after Luke left me, I realized I have a lot of things to decide on my own. I need to choose what I believe. What kind of person I want to be.

I don't tell them I'm pregnant—because yes, that's a huge part of this, but another part of me knows I need time away, otherwise I'm scared I'll never learn to stand on my own. And I need to learn how I'm going to raise three children.

Because even though Jaxon says he will help ... I know this is a duty he doesn't want. A duty he isn't prepared for.

JAX

Dean and I are outside, sitting on stumps, drinking our beer. I'm glad he's here, knows the truth—because, shit, that would be a fucking hard conversation to have over the phone.

"You think having her stay here is a bad idea?" I ask Dean.

"Fuck, I don't know. You've just never settled down. Never had a serious relationship. And now her living here, plus kids. I don't know, man—it's a lot."

"She's had a rough go of things. Her family's really conservative and she's jumpy as a doe. She needs some time to breathe. Staying here can help with that."

"That doesn't mean you marry her."

I choke on my motherfucking beer. "Marry her? Who said anything about getting married?"

"Dude, you know that's what she's angling for. I mean, why else would she wanna shack up at this piece of shit cabin with you? She wants you to commit, be more than a baby-daddy. She wants you to fucking propose."

"Well, that shit's not happening. Marriage is bullshit. You know how I feel about that. And I'll let Harper stay here until she has the kids, and then I can help pay for day care or something, get her set up in town. Where there will be people who can help her. That's a shit-ton of diapers."

"I think she's hoping you're gonna be the one changing those. I saw the way she looks at you. She thinks you're some kind of god."

"No way. She knows this is short-term. And yeah, she's hot, fucking amazing in bed ... but I'm not getting married. I don't even know her."

"And she knows this?"

"Fuck, Dean. She doesn't know anything She's sheltered, and has no real-life experience. And besides all that, we've spent like two days together. I know nothing about her intentions, and she knows less about mine."

"Well, then, this next month together, out here without any other person to lean on, you'll figure one another out pretty damn fast."

"Right. So I'll give it a month. Harper and I will know after that what we wanna do next. Her staying here doesn't equal us getting hitched. That ain't happening, bro."

"Hey, and before I go, we need to talk about money. We're going to expand D&J Hauling. Do you want in on that?"

"Who the fuck is *we*?"

"My new right-hand man, Thomas, and I. We want to start doing custom homes. We're hauling the best timber in the state, and we need to capitalize on it."

"Yeah, I'm in. I need to do something besides chopping fucking wood all day." We look around my acreage, and Dean lets out a low whistle.

"It's a shit-ton of wood, Jax." Dean says, impressed.

"I've been sending it to the mill once every

few weeks. Can you send a truck out here to get it for resale?"

"Sure. And I'll let you know about the expansion. Plan on coming by next month when you're in town for Harper's appointment."

After Dean leaves, Harper tells me she's exhausted and needs to nap. Once she's settled I head down the mountain to Buck's general store/post-office and connect to his Wi-Fi. I order a bunch of girly shit, mostly stuff Harper wrote down on a pad of paper for me, then I check my email, knowing I need to write my parents. There's a note waiting for me, from them. Apparently they're in their RV and headed back to Idaho for the summer.

I email them back. They should know I'm gonna be a fucking father.

Then I grab a basket and walk around the store to get basic stuff like a toothbrush and shampoo. I have a feeling Harper will to want to use something besides a bar of soap. I grab a few food items that I think will make Harper smile. And, shit, that girl needs a break. After she wrote the letter I swear she was flat-out drained.

Buck eyes my basket as I set it on the counter for him to ring up. "What's all this?"

"None of your damn business."

"It's a small town, Jax." Buck bags the ladies' deodorant, pursing his lips. "Guessing this shit's not for you."

"My friend is staying. Unexpectedly."

"You're off the market then? Because damn, boy, women are in here all the time asking about the guy who I was at the bar with a few weeks back."

I knew it was stupid to ever go out with Buck.

"I'm off the market. But to be clear, I was never on it to begin with."

"Whatever you say." When he gets to my food choices he looks at them and then back to me. Then looks at them again. "Pickles and ice-cream? Dude ... you have something you need to say?"

"Not to you, I don't."

Pay and leave. I just want to get back to Harper, and make sure she's doing okay.

It's not that I want to marry her—fuck no. I've hashed all that out with Dean. But I do want to make sure the woman carrying my children is going to be all right.

CHAPTER NINETEEN

HARPER

THAT FIRST NIGHT at Jaxon's I wake with a start. Looking around the loft where I was sleeping with him beside me, in his old tee shirt, his breathing heavy in my ear, I wonder if I made a series of terrible choices that will never get me back on the straight and narrow. Maybe I've fallen so far off the deep end that I'll never be able to climb back up and stand.

But then I place my hand on the bump beneath my navel, and I remember that being here in Jaxon's bed gives me comfort, a sense of peace, and that if I want to experience a smooth pregnancy, I need those things. I need them for my babies.

Jaxon unconsciously repositions himself,

deep in slumber, and wraps his arms around me. I let go of the breath I've been holding and close my eyes. In his arms I sleep; in his arms I dream of a life I never knew I might want, but suddenly have.

JAX

The first day she fried me eggs and made homemade biscuits.

The second day she baked me a dozen chocolate chip cookies.

The third day she whipped up meatloaf and mashed potatoes.

The fourth day she slid a pan of cinnamon rolls into the oven.

Today, the fifth day, I swear I've gained five pounds and tell her we need to drink smoothies or some shit.

She just laughs.

And then batters some chicken to fry.

HARPER

I may not know how to balance a checkbook or change the oil. But I do know how to cook and clean.

I polish every wood surface in that cabin. Which is saying an awful lot.

I wash the clothes, fold the clothes, put away the clothes.

I make the bed.

I bathe the dog, and brush him, too.

I spray Windex on the dirty windows, making them clear as the mountain days.

I watch Jaxon out of those newly cleaned windows.

Watch him chop wood, his shirt off, his muscles taut as he swings an axe over his shoulder.

Watch him wipe his brow with the corner of his shirt, wipe away sweat and dirt. Watch him stack piles of wood for the fire without pause.

It's usually at this point that I stop whatever chore I'm working on and beg him to come inside ... come inside me.

He always agrees.

He likes to whistle while drying dishes. He loves his dog and his mom and his dad. He is jealous that Dean gets to do what he wants in town and he hates that his choices landed him here.

He remembers dates precisely. He thinks Buck, the guy who delivers the boxes of clothes Jax ordered for me, is an asshat, for no real reason. He likes it when I belly laugh, and he kisses my stomach every night before we go to bed.

He doesn't press me about my plans, so I don't press him either.

He makes my heart pitter-patter when he nuzzles my neck. He makes me believe in the possibility of falling in love with a stranger who's suddenly become my entire world.

He watches me when he thinks I'm not looking.

There's a question on the tip of his tongue. A question he hasn't asked.

I'm scared he'll ask me something I don't want to answer.

I'm more scared that he won't ask me anything at all.

JAX

She likes to wake early and take long walks. She likes coffee with cream and showers not-too-hot. She likes the smell of the wood burning in the fireplace, and when Jameson curls up at her feet.

She hates cats. She hates seafood. She hates fighting.

I learned that the hard way when we were playing a game of motherfucking SCRABBLE, and I thought a word was a word that wasn't.

She doesn't know pop-culture references like Brangelina, any of the Beatles' songs, and has never watched Ghostbusters. She resents her sheltered childhood, but loves it when I explain the reasons Star Wars is so fucking great.

She is clueless and bewildered and beautiful and brave. She is over her head in a million ways and I have no clue how she's going to do this next part—raising three children—but she doesn't seem to shy away from expanding her world. I think the task is too large for even both of us, together.

She tells me of her church family. Of potlucks and bible studies and prayer meetings. She tells me how she memorized entire books of the bible and how her home was so full of people. How caring for them was her favorite thing to do.

I know she'll be a good mom, but she and I becoming a family? It seems impossible. There isn't enough time for us both to grow up enough to be all those things at once. Mother and father and husband and wife.

A few months ago I was a bad boy, run out of town, chopping motherfucking wood. She was a virgin, about to marry a man who planned on telling her how to dress, eat, sleep ... *be*.

I don't want to tell Harper what to do. That's not my fucking job.

Besides, she knows a lot of what she likes without me giving her any hints.

For example, she likes every position we fuck in.

So, I tickle her pussy with my beard until she drenches me with her juice.

I suck her clit until she gets wet all over me, and then I press my tongue in deeper until she pours out her release.

I kiss every inch of her skin until she writhes underneath me, begging me to fuck her.

I do.

Every day.

For four weeks straight.

CHAPTER TWENTY

HARPER

My stomach is getting slightly bigger, and it feels heavy. Weighted. Like there really are three people inside of me.

I'm sitting in a leather back chair by the fireplace, drinking a mug of chamomile tea, staring at the ultrasound shots for the millionth me. The edges are frayed and the corners bent, but the three babies are swimming on a black background, proving to me their existence.

"You still looking at those?" Jaxon asks, coming to sit next to me after his shower. He's been working outside all day with the men from the sawmill, who came up in their truck to haul a bunch of Jaxon's fallen logs.

He was covered in sweat earlier, but now he's clean.

"Yeah, just wanted to sit for a minute while dinner is cooking."

"Smells good," he says.

I shrug modestly. "Lasagna."

"Fancy."

"I guess. But you're getting low on supplies. Maybe after the doctor appointment tomorrow we can go to the grocery store?"

"Yeah, we could do something like that. It's gonna be a long day, though, Harper. Maybe we should stay in the city before we drive all the way back here."

"That's fine. Like, were you thinking we could maybe stay with Dean for the night?" I ask.

Jaxon coughs. "It can be longer than a night. I thought maybe you'd like to go home for a while? Your parents haven't seen you since you told them you were pregnant. Maybe they'd like to spend time with you? I could meet them and make sure they know I'm not some creep in the woods."

I look back at the ultrasound. Swallow hard. Jaxon thinks I told them about the triplets in the letter I'd sent. But I didn't. Of course I didn't. And still, after a month together, Jaxon doesn't seem to understand that my parents aren't going to be forgiving. They won't let me back home without begging for forgiveness. They won't bring me back into the fold unless I repent.

And I don't want to repent right now. Right now, I want to be here. With Jaxon.

"Are you trying to get me to leave? Because I don't want to overstay my welcome." I know my tone is sharp, but I don't know how to be soft when his words feel like jagged lines, cutting over my heart.

He lifts his hands in defense, as if backtracking before he has even begun. "Of course you can stay, Harper. I just mean, this past month you've been playing house here, and its sort of make-believe. Maybe you should go home and face the facts."

"This isn't real?" I ask, looking at the small stretch of space between us. I thought we were knitting ourselves together for the past month, that our care and devotion for one another was growing ... but maybe it was all one-sided.

Which feels impossible to believe. It has been real when I put my mouth on his cock, when I spread open my legs and arched my back.

"Even if we were in love, Harper, you and I can't raise three babies on our own. We're way over our heads. At some point we're going to need to start making a plan that involves the help of other people."

My heart stills, ignoring the responsible words Jaxon says. Words like *plan* and *help*. I don't hear those right now. I'm stuck on his first sentence.

"You don't love me, then?" I ask. I want him to proclaim his devotion, promise and make vows. I want him to be something he never said he would be.

But still, I hoped.

"Harper," Jax starts, running his hand over his beard. "I'm trying, here."

"Haven't you loved this past month? Loved the time we've spent together?"

"Yeah, it's been good."

I can't help but let a small laugh escape my lips. "It's been *good*? What am I ... just someone you sleep with? Because I really thought that this thing between us was more than that."

"You want me to make promises I'm not ready to make."

"What are you ready for, Jaxon?" I ask. "Because it doesn't sound like you're ready for anything."

"I'm ready for this conversation to be over. I never should have started it. You don't have to go to your parents, I would never make you do something you didn't want to do."

Studying Jaxon's face, I don't quite believe his sudden change of heart.

I stand, go to the kitchen and take the lasagna from the oven. "Let's enjoy this evening and try to relax," I say, longing to get back to the place where we laughed and smiled and lived in the moment. "Tomorrow we'll find out the gender of these babies and we can talk about what comes next then."

Jaxon lets out a sigh. "Good God, woman, thank you for dropping it. For now."

"How did you plan on thanking me?" I tease, pulling the hot pan from the oven. "Because this is going to need to cool down for thirty minutes."

"Plenty of time for a thank you," he says, crossing the room to me. He pulls me into an embrace, and my shoulders fall, my eyes close. I want to sink into this feeling of bliss.

Even if I know we're using sex to distract us from reality ... right now, I want to melt away.

JAX

Holding Harper in my arms feels so right, but I swear there's something she isn't telling me, isn't being honest about. I'm surprised her family hasn't come out here all month to check on her and the pregnancy ... and that's why I mentioned that we should go over there tomorrow.

There's no way in hell we can have these kids without at least some sort of support. We need to get her parents on board. My parents are driving across the country, and should be here soon, but they don't live here.

"Kiss me," Harper whispers, tugging my mouth to hers. I give in to her kisses, her hand reaching toward the bulge in my pants. How could I not? Harper is beautiful and my cock grows as she grinds against me. So much of Harper is perfect ... but that doesn't mean she and I should build an entire life together. It still feels like too much, too soon.

"Jaxon, are you okay? Are you here?" Harper asks.

"I'm here, honey." I blink back the thoughts running through my mind. The reality of this situation is fucking with my head.

"Good." Harper smiles, lowers herself to the floor, kneeling before me. She reaches for the buttons on my jeans and tugs them down. "You certainly are here."

My cock is released from my boxers and is eager for Harper's attention. She has no problem giving it. In a moment her mouth begins to widen as she takes the tip of my cock.

Looking up at me, those gorgeous doe eyes of hers are bright and alive.

I feel like an ass for mentioning her family. She's such a sweet, generous woman, and I'm a dick for causing her any pain. For bringing up those assholes that raised her.

She takes me deeper and my cock is solid and hard for her as she sucks me.

"That's nice," I say, as she takes my balls in her hand, massaging them as she dips her head up and down over my rod. I want her clothes off, I want to see her nice perky tits, her hard nipples, and her dripping pussy.

She keeps sucking me off, harder and harder, so nice and good. A month of practice, and Harper knows exactly what to do. Her hands wraps around my shaft as she licks my tip all the way to the base. My whole cock is slick and ready to slide into her tight pussy.

"I want to be in you, honey," I tell her as she deep-throats me. She doesn't stop; she keeps taking me, the tip of my cock hitting the back of her throat, until I'm ready to explode in her wet mouth.

I thrust into her willing mouth and come hard and fast as she moans in pleasure. She loves swallowing my come, loves taking my seed in her mouth.

She pops my massive cock out of her mouth,

her lips swollen and eyes glistening with her mounting pleasure. She wants me to fuck her until her legs shake, and I will.

"Will you come in me again?" she asks, standing, her hand still cupping my balls, leaning down to kiss them like she can't get enough. She loves to fondle me; it gets her nice and wet when she does.

"Fuck yeah, I will," I tell her, pulling her to me and devouring her mouth. I kiss her hard and with desire. My tongue circles hers, and my still-hard cock pushes at her pussy. My lips trail kisses down her neck, her chest. I tear off her top, and my rod grows harder looking at her perfect tits wrapped up in that red lacy bra. I had fun picking out clothes for her online, bras and panties dripping with lace and netting. Not to mention the crotchless thongs.

Like the pair she is wearing right now.

Stepping away, I push down her pants, revealing that nicely shaven pussy. Since she moved here, her hair has gotten shorter and shorter, until she decided to go completely bare. I like it bare, because that way I can get a better view of her nice pussy lips, her opening when it's slick with desire, ready for me to fuck her. Or, better, for me to watch her finger fuck herself.

"Touch yourself," I tell her, slapping her ass.

"Over on the rug. I want to watch you make yourself wet.

"I'm already dripping," she says.

"I want to watch you gush, and I want to lick up all that juice."

She follows my request and sashays to the bearskin rug. Oh her back, her hair splayed out over her shoulders, her tits big and round, her stomach bump perfect, too. She bites her lip, her hands massaging those fucking perfect globes, thumbing her own nipples as she moans. Her legs spread for me, and I get on my knees before her, my hard cock twitching with excitement as I eye her opening.

Then she pushes two fingers between the fabric of the crotchless panties. The slit is nice and big so I can see everything she does. I could easily rip them off her, but I like watching as she presses her fingers between the silky material, as if she's reaching for something forbidden, something she shouldn't have. I watch as she moves her finger in and out, and then, as her excitement increases, she uses the middle finger of her other hand to massage the top of her opening. That's when she starts to soak my rug. That's when her hand moves faster and faster as she works to orgasm. Her tight little pussy is so wet, and I can't help myself.

I need to lick her dry.

I tear off her panties, press my head between her legs and kiss at the soft skin of her inner thighs. Trying to torture her playfully, I kiss around her pussy. Her hands reach for my hair, and she massages my scalp and she begs me to suck her.

"Not yet, honey."

I kiss her softly, using my hands to reach around to her ass, my fingers grazing her opening, but refusing to go in. When I know she's desperate, because she's moaning louder, I use my tongue to make a nice long lick right up the middle of her. Tracing her lips with my tongue, I watch her settle in ecstasy, her moaning turning to whispers.

I start sucking on her perfect little lips, so tender and ripe. My tongue circles her clit, darts up and down her entrance, teasing her with my pulsing. She loves it, tries to wiggle away because the pleasure is too good, too much. I won't let her get away.

I grip my hands around her smooth legs, and bury my head in her pussy. Eating her out tastes so good and I press my lips into her harder, savoring her juice as her pussy begs for more. I use two fingers and feather them against her insides, lightly flicking until shivers cover her skin.

I grind my face against her entrance, and I

know she's so close. Her legs press against me, asking for more, harder and deeper, so I give her what she wants. I press three fingers into her, fucking her fast, as she starts squirting all over me, her juice fucking pouring on my hand. My cock throbs, wanting her pussy lips wrapped around me tight.

I spread her legs wider, pounding her pussy with my hand; she rocks under me as the orgasm pushes through her. I flip her over, wanting her on her hands and knees as I fuck her hard. Her ass is right in my face—so round, and ready for a good spanking.

I slap her ass and she moans in pleasure. "Get in me, Jaxon, please. Now. I need you in me."

She's right. She does need a good pounding. So I press my cock into her opening, as she's bending for me. I grip her ass and thrust into her nice and good. Hard. She groans in delight and I thrust again, rocking her deep and good. Her tight pussy can take me now without her gasping because she knows that when I get in her, nice and deep, she's going to come. And that orgasm is always worth the momentary pain of my massive cock in her.

"Oh, Jaxon, oh baby, oh yeah," she moans as I thrust again, spraying my come deep inside her pussy walls.

I hold onto her hips, loving her skin up against me. She sits up, my cock still in her. I hold her gorgeous tits in my hands; they're so big and beautiful my hands can't even hold them completely. I press them together, her ass grinding on my lap, her head rolling back in my shoulders.

"I love you, Jaxon," she whispers.

I kiss the soft skin of her neck, not knowing how to say the words she wants to hear. I can't say them if part of me still thinks I might say good-bye.

CHAPTER TWENTY-ONE

HARPER

We drive into the city without hitting any speed bumps, and I reach for Jaxon's hand as we walk into the clinic. The appointment with Doctor Vance starts off rocky. First, she gives Jaxon a once over, and I realize that, in the fluorescent light of the office, he looks even burlier than he does out in the woods. His beard and tattoos, his rugged clothes and edgy eyes, give off a don't-mess-with-me vibe. Which isn't exactly inviting.

Doctor Vance regroups quickly and professionally, greeting us both with handshake, though she's quick to explain that she was disappointed with me for never following through with a counseling appointment. But I don't need a counselor anymore. Because I'm in love with Jaxon and we are going to have a life together, and my family can hate me, but it doesn't matter.

Because Jaxon can be my family now.

Which I know is maybe setting myself up for disappointment ... but surely once we find out the gender of the babies this will seem more real to him—cause him to realize we need each other to get through this next part. He thinks I need my parents, but I don't. He will be enough.

"All right, Harper, if you're still feeling well, then we will stay the course. Your blood pressure reads normal, and your weight gain is steady. I couldn't be more pleased with this. So far, it's best-case scenario. So now we need to start talking about any screenings you'd like done for the babies."

"I don't want any testing done." I shake my head. Even being here with a doctor, instead of a midwife, goes against my first choice.

"But what if it helps?" Jaxon asks.

"No," I say. "It's not even up for debate. I want everything as natural as possible."

"Even the delivery?" Jaxon asks.

"Of course. I don't believe in medical intervention. What will be, will be."

Jaxon and Doctor Vance exchange a look.

"What?" I ask. "Don't do that ... that thing where you look at one another and judge me."

"No one is judging anyone," Doctor Vance says, reaching out to pat my arm.

"That's not true," Jaxon says, scoffing at the doctor's words. "I think it's insane to not find out everything we can about the babies before they're born. And I also think it's ridiculous to think you're going to deliver them without any medical assistance. What if there's a problem, Harper? You would just let the babies die?"

Flustered I answer, "Of course not. But. I don't know. I want to trust that everything happens for a reason."

"That's the stupidest thing I've ever heard." Jaxon crosses his arms, shaking his head at me. "Happens for a reason? You think there's a reason we're here, having three kids? There is no reason for that. No bigger meaning. It was a one-night stand that went wrong. Way wrong. It was nothing but a huge mistake, Harper."

Tears fill my eyes. He thinks, after the last month we spent together, that this is wrong? *Still?*

But I see it as so right. I see him and me, opposites in so many ways, but I thought maybe our differences are what could make us great. Make us a family.

"Should we schedule an appointment with a

mediator?" Doctor Vance asks, a finger hovering over her tablet as she listens to our fight. "Often times pregnancy becomes a very large stressor in a relationship. And this is a multiples pregnancy, which could have even more triggers for heated conversations."

"I don't think this is a relationship, Doctor," I say. Sniffling, I refuse to look at Jaxon. Not if everything we just experienced together, sleeping in the same bed, sharing meals, and sharing ourselves, was meaningless. "And I don't think we're going to be needing the ultrasound, after all."

She cocks her head to the side in confusion. "Harper, besides determining the gender, we'll be able to get a good look at the babies' organs to make sure everything is as it should be."

"No. I don't want that today. It's too much, too intrusive. I didn't even think about the fact that the ultrasound was a way of playing God, but it is."

"This is a God issue now?" Jaxon asks, incredulous.

"Maybe it always was, Jaxon. Luke broke off our engagement because he didn't think I was holy enough, devoted enough. And at the time, I was so angry at that assessment of me. But was he so far off? Look at me—at who I've become since I met you."

"Fuck this," Jaxon says, hands raised in defeat.

"Okay, Jaxon, let's give Harper space to dress." She opens the door and shoos him out. Then, turning to me, she says, "You okay? Is there someone you'd like me to call?"

"There's no one for you to call," I tell her.

When she shuts the door, I fall apart. I'm not strong enough to cry with anyone; right now I am weak. Right now I am nothing but alone and it is all my fault.

JAX

I've been upset with women. Plenty of them. And even just coming back into this city reminds me of what I was doing down here, *who* I was doing down here.

I was tense before I walked into the doctor's clinic. And then when Doctor Vance scanned me head-to-toe, telling herself I was everything she didn't want—when we both know I am exactly what she wants—I wanted out of the appointment, stat.

But I wasn't looking to get out of whatever-the-hell Harper and I are. I admit, I'm head-fucked about how to proceed. Do I just marry her to make her happy? Because part of me thinks that would be easiest. Maybe we get a house back here, I get a respectable position with whatever Dean's new enterprise is. Work nine-to-five and come home to my wife and kids.

I mean, do I want that? Hell, no. But I'm not an asshole. I got this woman pregnant. A woman who happens to be fucking hot in bed, adorable when she cooks me dinner, and a dick tease when she slinks around my cabin in my tee shirt and nothing else. It's not that I don't want to keep banging Harper—I just know at the end of the day she wants more than a good screw. She wants forever.

And, fuck, that isn't something I'm prepared to give. But maybe I'm just being a stubborn fool. Fact is, it's not gonna get much better than Harper. She is more than a solid ten, she gets my cock hard without trying, she's the mother of my children—and I may not be religious, but I swear she's heaven on Earth.

But then that shit went down in the doctor's office, and I have no clue what Harper wants. It's like she wants it both ways: to have me, but also keep her morals. I can't fucking offer her Jesus Christ. I can only give her myself. And if she really wants a life with me, I think that should be enough.

In the hallway, Doctor Vance speaks more candidly than she did in the room with Harper.

"Jaxon, I've only met Harper once before," she says. "But I wonder about her level of support ... if maybe there is someone else in her life she can rely on?"

"I don't know," I say, swallowing. "I don't know her that well. I've never met her family. Every time I mention support she gets all tense, and I hate to see her that way."

"I know there is no easy answer, especially when a pregnancy occurs in a new relationship. Regardless of her decision for the ultrasound, I will see her in a month, and hopefully I'll be seeing you again as well."

In the car with Harper, I want to tell her everything is going to be okay. Somehow. My parents will be arriving soon, and I'm not a mama's boy by any means, but I do know my parents are solid and will help however they can.

Shit, after I sent them an email letting them know about the triplets, my mom convinced my dad that they needed to spend the winter in Idaho.

And I know it's a bad time to propose, after our biggest fight, but I need to settle this with her, so we can make a fucking plan. The babies are coming whether or not we have one, and I may have a history, but I have no intention of being a deadbeat father.

"Harper," I say, facing her in the car. "We need to talk about what happened in there."

"Stop," she says. "I just want to go home."

"Harper, we drove all day, we need to eat and grocery shop. I've gotta talk to Dean. I'm not driving back to the cabin right now."

"Not your cabin. Home. I want you to take me to my parents."

"You were dead set against it."

"Things change, Jaxon. I need to be with people who understand me."

"I thought the problem was they wouldn't understand. Wouldn't accept."

"I have to give them a chance to accept me, okay?"

"They could have come all month to see you, check on you and the babies. They chose to stay away."

"No," Harper says, shaking her head. "I never told them about the pregnancy. I told them not to come to the cabin."

I sigh, frustrated that Harper would be so ... so .... Looking at her, I know exactly what she was. What she is. So scared.

"Fine, I'll come with you, introduce myself, and help you explain."

"Explain what, exactly, Jaxon? Explain that I

broke all my covenants? All my promises? That I am exactly the girl Luke accused me of being? Tell them that I'm with you, a man who doesn't even want to do the honorable thing and marry me?"

"We're talking about honor, now?" I pound my fist on the steering wheel. The horn blasts, and I want to scream. "I'm doing everything I can to take care of you, Harper. Just fucking give me a chance."

I will marry her. And it isn't about honor. It's about wanting to be with her. Her smile and laugh and love. I want Harper, but now she won't hear me, hear any of it. She'll think its a last-ditch effort. And maybe it is. Maybe I needed to get to this place, rock bottom, to realize that I want her.

"Let me be the man you need."

"I don't want that. Not now. I just want to go home."

HARPER

Jaxon pulls up to my parents' home, and I see him move to unbuckle. I put my hand on his.

"Please, stay in the car."

"I have to come in with you, to explain this."

"I think my stomach will explain enough."

"Fuck that."

"Stop it, Jaxon. You can't force your way in there."

"For you I can."

"No. I don't want to be with you. Not like this. Not anymore. Just listen to me. Believe me. Just go," I say, my words forceful and direct.

A shadow crosses Jaxon's face. I'm breaking him.

"We're too different," I tell him, trying to ease him away. I see tears fill his eyes, and they fill mine too, and I can't believe I am doing this. "You will always see me as inferior, as stupid and naive. And I will always wonder if I trapped you in a relationship you don't want. Be honest with yourself, be honest with me. You don't want this."

"Your dad might do something crazy. He might hurt you. Or throw you out. I can't drive away not knowing if you're fucking okay."

"I'm not asking you again. I need to go," I yell at him, pushing open the door of his truck.

"Harper, don't leave like this. This isn't a game. This is our life. Harper!" Jaxon screams my name. He gets out of the car, runs toward me. I take off for the house, needing familiar. Needing my family. Praying they will be comforting and not condemning. Praying they will accept, not deny.

Tears stream down my cheeks. The front

door opens. My parents walk outside just as I run toward them. I am desperate to feel safe. Feel known.

But before I take another step, I trip on the rockery. Fall. Clutching my stomach, I tumble to the ground.

The world spins. Then it stops.

And everything is black.

CHAPTER TWENTY-TWO

HARPER

WHEN I WAKE UP, an IV is connected to my arm; a fetal monitor is strapped to my stomach. I'm in a hospital gown, and a screen records the *thumpthumpthump* of the babies' heartbeats.

They are alive. I am alive. Oh, my heart—I'd thought, as I fell, it was all over.

I blink back tears, press my hands to my growing belly. We're okay. My babies and me, at least. Because I don't know if there is anyone else left.

Jaxon's rumbling voice, calling out my name, asking me to stay with him in the car, rings through my head as I remember what happened before I tripped and fell.

I told Jaxon we were done. We fought at the

doctor appointment. We're too different, from different worlds, with different dreams—and he never asked for me to stay, to be his. He agreed to let me live at his cabin after I pushed my way in.

This housewife-game I've been playing at all month was a one-sided daydream that ended with me in a hospital bed, waking up from a nightmare.

"Harper, you're awake." A nurse in pale pink scrubs, her dark hair tied back, enters the room. She walks over to the monitor tracking everything happening within my womb. "You've been here several hours, but we had you sedated to let you recover in your own time from the trauma."

"I see the three heartbeats," I say, pointing to the monitor where three heartbeats are being tracked. "That means all three babies are okay, right?"

"You are a very lucky mama," the nurse says, repositioning a monitor on my stomach. "All three are doing very well. Look at him, there, he is just happy as a clam."

"He?"

"Mmmhhmm," the nurse says absently as she prints some records off the machine that's tracking the babies' and my heart rate. "I'm sure everyone says it, but you will be such a busy mother. Three babies is one thing, but three boys? You are a saint!"

"Three boys?" My voice catches, and I don't hide it. "I'm having three boys?"

"You didn't know? Oh, sweetie, I'm so sorry. I assumed you knew. It's routine with a multiple pregnancy that everyone involved has a very clear picture of the babies."

I felt overwhelmed before ... but now? Now I need what I was looking for when I fled Jaxon's car. Comfort. Familiar. I need family.

"Is anyone here for me?"

"Yes, there are quite a few people waiting. Looks like you come from a big family yourself. Your parents are here, along with quite a few children. And the father is here too."

"My father?"

"No, I'm pretty sure the man, Jaxon, is the father of your children. He's been pacing the hospital for three hours, signing releases on behalf of the babies. He's a nervous wreck, to be honest."

"Can I see them?"

"The doctor is on her way. So first I need you to speak with Doctor Vance, then you can see your family."

As if on cue, Doctor Vance walks in, tablet in hand.

"Harper," she clucks. "I should never have let you walk away today."

"I'm just glad the babies are okay," I say quietly. "And I hear they're three boys?"

She smiles softly, pulling up a chair and then sitting beside me. The nurse leaves the room, and I release a deep sigh, sure I am about to be reprimanded, and with good reason. I've been irresponsible in thousand different ways.

"While you were recovering, we did ultrasounds on the triplets, and are so relieved to know they sustained zero impact from the fall. And you're in perfect health, which is helping tremendously as you carry three babies."

"But...?" I frown, knowing there is always a but.

"But your stress levels are too high. You can't continue to term if you're so unsettled, so up in the air. It sounds like the family doesn't know about the high-risk pregnancy, and you and the triplets' father don't appear to be on the same page."

"High-risk pregnancy?

"A multiple birth pregnancy is inherently high-risk, Harper. I know having triplets can appear exciting, but there's a huge responsibility added to this situation."

"I don't know what I'm supposed to do."

"Well, first thing I suggest is make a plan

with your support. That seems to be your parents and partner. After that, we can debrief on the plan and I will need to determine if, as the health care provider, it sounds feasible before I can discharge you. I think a good step would be conversations with both parties, and then everyone together."

I nod, knowing that what she suggests happens next is the scary part. Talking to Jaxon. And my parents. In the same room, at the same time. The thing I put my children at risk to avoid.

I will never be so selfish again.

Even if it means I'm doing this next part—raising these sons—all alone.

JAX

I watched the Doctor walk in Harper's fucking room. That tells me she's awake, and it also tells me that the hospital bullshit I've been fed all day is just about over. They told me I'd be able to see her once she was awake.

I fought them on that; I should be able to sit in there with Harper and the babies. My children. My motherfucking family. But they said no.

Granted, Harper decided she doesn't quite see me that way. Which is just another piece of bullshit red tape I have to cut through to get what I want.

What I fucking need.

Harper back in my arms, our children growing between us.

I need to make her understand that, yeah, this started as a one-night stand. And yeah, I don't want to be a father right now. But I am, and I can be more. I need to show her that.

A nurse walks past me—a nurse I know I screwed in the bathroom at Mo's Bar downtown. Twice. Of course I have to see that shit at the same time I'm pacing the halls alongside Harper's father.

Did I mention her entire family is here? And yeah. They are pissed.

But, honestly, I fucking get it.

Their oldest daughter ran away a month ago, not telling them shit besides she was off screwing some guy in the woods.

I'm glad her father never showed up to try and chew me out, but, shit—I know he has a few choice words for me. He's been stewing for hours, his wife looking at me from head to fucking toe. Probably judging me on all the ways this situation is messed up.

Her siblings, all nine of them, are sitting quietly with heads bowed, whispering. Not one is running around or arguing or fighting. Her family may be leaning toward the crazy side, but they're sure as hell well-behaved.

I need to man up and go talk to her parents. Because the last thing I want is to get in a room with them—with Harper—and fight. Harper doesn't need that, and neither do the babies.

I run my hand through my hair, over my beard. Nervous tics that are boyish bullshit. I need to be a fucking man.

I pull back my shoulders, swallow hard. Crack my neck. I can go over there and introduce myself. This isn't fucking rocket science.

"Hey," I say to her father. "I'm Jaxon."

He nods his head stoically. "I'm Reverend Robert. This is my wife, Shelly." He pauses, then offers me his hand. The handshake is weak, but at least it's a fucking handshake. An olive branch or whatever religious bullshit this guy is gunning for. Whatever. I'll take it.

For Harper, I'll take anything.

I should have fucking told her that back at my cabin, or in the doctor's office. In my car. I should have stopped being such a pig-headed fool, and never let her run away from me. She's here right now in a hospital bed because I was an ass. A real man would never have let it come to this. Sure, she's having my kids, but she's also the only woman I ever fucking want.

She's soft in the ways I'm hard, and curious

in the ways I'm cold. She's resilient in the ways I run, and I'm strong in the ways she's scared. We fucking belong together. And I need her to know that.

"Good to meet you both." I cough as a way to pause, wanting to make sure I get it right. "Obviously, Harper has been at my place all month. I assume you got the letter from Dean?"

Robert nods again. "Dean came by a month ago, yes. Seemed like a nice fellow."

"And the letter? He gave you that?"

"He did. Did you read it first?"

"No, sir," I answer, suddenly a fucking diplomat. Since when did I fucking care about being polite?

Oh, right—about the time Harper was admitted in the Emergency Room. About the time I nearly lost everything.

That fall in her parents' front yard could have been so much worse. She could have landed face down. She could have lost all the babies. Instead, everyone survived.

She calls this pregnancy a fucking miracle?

I call *her* a miracle. And I call her mine.

"She wrote some pretty disappointing things, Jaxon. Questioned her entire faith, her values. Her moral integrity. She questioned them, and—at the same time, apparently—hid a pregnancy from us."

"I thought you knew," I tell them.

"We didn't."

Robert looks at Shelly, whose eyes are rimmed in tears. I hope—shit, I'm not a praying man, but I pray he redeems himself right about now, for Harper's sake. She ran from the car today hoping this family of hers would give her what she needed, something familiar and something safe.

I pray they can fucking deliver.

Robert speaks again, "This afternoon has been shocking. Losing our daughter to the sins of the world, to a man like you, is one thing. But to know she is bringing life into a life of sin? It's unbearable to accept that she would choose such a deplorable future for her offspring. That she would choose a man of this world over eternity with her family."

"That is fucking bullshit, sir," I tell him, not able to hold back. "You think Harper is a sinner? A fucking disgrace? She's a fucking angel. So don't stand here and talk about her like she's dirty. Because she's not. She's as pure as a doe. She is nothing to be ashamed of. And to say that here, when she's in the hospital, is goddamned crazy."

Robert clenches his jaw, disgust written on his face.

"Don't speak such vile words to me," he says,

his lips pursed in hate. "Don't say such filth in front of my children and wife. Harper has chosen to live the life of a whore. She has chosen a man like you, with a reputation like you have, over a pious life in the church."

"My words are vile? You're the one calling your daughter names—a woman who is brave and strong. You're the one calling a woman who is fucking beautiful something dirty. Fuck you—fuck all of you," I shout.

I want to punch him. To bruise him. I want to hurt him, because he's a fucking pig. A man I never want to see again. A man I never want my children near. I need Harper. And I need her now. I need her to know the truth. That I'm not going anywhere.

Not now, not ever.

"Excuse me, everyone." Doctor Vance materializes as I'm neck-to-neck with Robert.

I step back, trying to calm the fuck down. But, damn, it's hard. I want to punch that asshole until he spins.

Doctor Vance speaks again, "Harper is ready to see you all. I think, at this time, it would probably be best if you go in two separate groups. I know you're all anxious to see her, but she and I have just spoken and made a tentative plan. She needs to speak with everyone separately, and then hopefully everyone together."

I step forward. "Can I go in now?"

"Actually, Harper has requested to speak with her parent first," Doctor Vance says. "How about you go get some food from the cafeteria and come back in, say, an hour?"

I want to scream, fight, say no. But I need to let Harper be the woman she is, speak with who she needs to speak with. It's not like her fucking father's true feelings are going to be masked.

I'll be here when she's ready.

If she needs an hour, fine. I know exactly how I'm going to spend it.

I leave the hospital, leave her parents, because I want nothing to do with them. And I pray Harper doesn't either.

CHAPTER TWENTY-THREE

HARPER

I WAIT IN SILENCE, knowing that, as soon as the door opens and my parents walk in, everything will either fall into place or fall apart. This is the moment I've been dreading, ever since I confirmed this pregnancy. The moment I know will define my future and the future of my children. My sons.

"Harper." My father enters the room, my mother trailing behind him.

His eyes cast a shadow over the room. They're heavy with pain, with sorrow. I know this look. I've seen him lift up the needs of his congregation, carry their burdens, help them walk toward salvation and toward light. But while those congregants end their journeys with a new sense of peace and righteousness, they always start on their knees, broken.

I need my parents to see that while I detoured from their plan for me—from God's will—I ended up on their doorstep for a reason.

"I'm sorry for leaving," I say, my eyes on my stomach, not able to bear looking at them. I've felt their condemnation before. Right now, I just need their love—but I'm scared it won't be offered.

"What else are you sorry for?" my father asks, standing at the end of the hospital bed. My mother is beside him; she covers her mouth with her hand, clearly in shock to see me like this.

"You want me to apologize right now?" I ask, caught off guard. My eyebrows furrow.

"Yes. You are a sinner," Father says, "and if you want to return to the fold, we need to know you intend on walking the straight and narrow path the Lord requires."

I open my mouth to speak, but then snap it shut. What am I supposed to say?

"Have you nothing more to say for your depravity?"

"Did the doctor tell you about the babies, then?"

"Babies?" my mom asks. "There are more than one?"

"The doctor only told us that you were well, and that the pregnancy was intact," my father says.

"I'm having triplets," I tell them. "Three sons."

My parents gasp at this information—and, considering they walked in here demanding my repentance, it's nice to see them grappling for words.

"Can I be a single mother in your congregation?" I ask my father. "Because I wonder how I can be both? A follower of the God you preach and also a mother raising a family on her own."

"I'm so disappointed in you," he answers, without offering anything concrete. "Your brothers and sisters are here praying for your repentance, your healing—and here you are, questioning our faith."

"I'm not questioning you," I say, shaking my head. "I'm trying to understand. Can I believe in your God, and also be grateful that I have these babies? Because I am. I was coming to your home earlier to tell you how much I need your support, your love. Because I can't do this on my own."

"You want our help now? After you've spent a month living in sin with that despicable man? I don't even know who you are, Harper. No daughter of mine would act this way."

"I am your daughter. These babies don't change that."

"These children change everything," my mother says. "You are no longer pure or chaste."

"Do you hear yourselves?" I ask, incredulous. "I stayed at Jaxon's because I was terrified of your response. And I was right in running. You aren't being a safe haven; you're not allowing God to be a beacon, a refuge. You're only offering condemnation and hate."

"That is what sinners say, when they don't want to look in the mirror."

"No," I say. My eyes close as I determine the precise words I need to use here. "I can look in the mirror and accept the woman I am, the woman I became when I got pregnant, and the woman I want to be as a mother. It doesn't seem like you're interested in a relationship with me unless it's exactly on your terms."

"Not my terms, Harper," my father yells. "The terms the Lord has laid out. Repent, and return to the fold. To your family. Your sons will be bastards in this world, but they can still be children of God."

"Go." My teeth grind on the fuel their words have given me. "Leave and don't come back. Not for me. I am done with your hate message. I am *done* with your hypocrisy. I wanted to give you a chance to love me and my children, but you aren't capable of that sort of love. The kind of love I have for Jaxon. Love that sees beyond differences and accepts the other person for who they are. You can't do that. But I can. I'm glad I'm not like you, because if I were, I wouldn't see so clearly how much I love the man who is the father of my sons."

"The man who just stormed out of the hospital?" my father asks, sneering at me in disgust.

"He left?"

"Yes. And we are, too."

"Mother, is this how you want things to end with me?" I ask. "Don't you want to know your grandsons? Know me?"

My mother, with her long braid and plain clothes and flat expression, looks at me. "I don't want to know you if you can't repent, Harper. I'd rather pretend you never existed than to acknowledge I'm a mother to someone like you."

They leave and don't look back. No hugs or well wishes, no how-can-we-help. Nothing. It's as if I'm not their daughter.

And, after they go, I wonder if I ever was. Because how could anyone turn their back on their child like they just did to me?

I will never turn my back on my sons.

My chin quivers as I'm left alone in the

sterile hospital room. Jaxon left without saying good-bye, and my heart is shattered, but I am also not surprised. I told him to go. I'm the one who left first. I deserve to be alone now.

But I don't want to be alone. I wish I never asked him to return to my parent's home. Going there forced us apart.

And all I want now is for us to be together.

JAX

I meet up with Dean downtown at The King's Diamond jewelry store. I park my truck outside, and I'm leaning against it with my hands in my pockets when he pulls up next to me.

"Now, this is a sight I never thought I'd fucking see," Dean says, jumping out of his truck. "You really feel like you need to do this?"

"I don't need to. I want to."

"Shit." Dean claps me on my back. "Then you need go get your woman a ring."

"I've got an hour. And I need you to tell me about the business—and I have a proposition for you, too."

We walk into the shop, and immediately I lower my head. "Fuck, see that woman over there?" I ask Dean. "We need to stay clear of her."

"Someone you never called back?"

"Exactly." Coming back to town, seeing the familiar nurse and now this jeweler, I'm reminded more than ever why I live in the woods. And why I need to stay there.

I wonder what Harper will think of that?

Fuck. I sure don't know everything I should about the woman I'm proposing to. I just hope she says yes, that she believes me when I tell her I want this ... not because of duty, but because of belief. Belief in what we can be, together.

"What about this one?" Dean asks, pointing to a gaudy ring that is nothing like Harper. It's an enormous solitaire on a silver band.

Harper needs something modest, delicate, and timeless. She wouldn't want anything else.

A woman that I haven't slept with helps me choose one that is perfect for Harper. It's a simple gold band, but the diamonds are rich with meaning.

"Man, you've become a fucking romantic sap, out in the woods," Dean jokes as we leave the shop. "I thought you were supposed to get all burly and tough."

"I know, right?" I shake my head. "Harper is everything I never knew I needed."

"Well, I'm happy for you. Now you wanna talk business?"

We stand at our trucks, and I know I need

to get a better sense of where things are with D&J Hauling.

"Yeah. You moving forward with the custom houses?"

"Yeah, no orders yet, but I need to figure out marketing for it. My buddy keeps saying to use Facebook ads or some shit and I want to punch him for that suggestion. Got any better ideas?"

"I have one idea for a potential client."

"I'm all ears."

When I walk back into the cold, antiseptic hospital corridor, I'm already itching to return to the cabin, to the smell of the wood stove and my dog. Buck kept him for the night, and he'll be well taken care of, but I want to be home with my dog and my woman.

I see Doctor Vance at the nurse's station, and I check in there before walking into Harper's room.

"Is it all clear for me to see her?"

"Oh, good, you're back. Her family left about half an hour ago, so I'm sure she'll be pleased to see you." Doctor Vance smiles kindly, which is nice considering the nurse beside her has furrowed brows and crossed arm. Ouch. Okay, just gotta keep walking forward.

I knock gently on the door to Harper's room before walking in. A curtain hangs between the entrance and her bed.

"Harper, is it okay for me to come in?"

"Jaxon?" she asks. "Of course, come in."

I pull back the curtain and see a tear-stained face. Harper's innocence is gone. She doesn't look naïve anymore. She looks like a wounded deer, and I want to kill whoever did this to her.

"What happened?" I ask, rushing over to her, sitting on her bed. My hands instinctively move to her beautiful, swollen belly.

"My parents...." She sobs into her hands. "They acted just like I thought they would. They left and said I wasn't their daughter. That my babies and I were a disgrace."

"Oh, honey." I shush her, wanting her tears to stop flowing. I want to protect her and take her far away, somewhere safe, I need to make sure no one can ever hurt her again.

My chest tightens, then expands in a way it never has before. This is love, right here: wanting to fight, defend, protect another person. And I'll fucking make it my life's mission to make sure no one ever fucks with Harper again.

"I know they're wrong. I know I have nothing to be ashamed of. I'm growing people inside of me, and that's a miracle. That they would shame me, when I'm being brave, hurts in a way I didn't think was possible. And then ... the worst part was ... I thought...." She dissolves in a puddle of tears again, and I reach for her hand.

She squeezes it tight.

"I thought you were gone, Jaxon. They said you left the hospital, and I thought it meant you'd left me, just like my parents left."

"I'll never fucking leave you, Harper."

"Don't say things you don't mean, Jaxon. My heart can't bear any more pain."

"I do mean it. I mean more. I mean *forever*."

Harper shakes her head, not understanding.

Knowing what I came here prepared to do, I drop to one knee and look up at Harper in her hospital gown, with her swollen eyes and broken heart. Look at the woman heavy with my children. Look at the woman who rocked my world, who changed the course of my life for the better. All I want is to look at her forever.

"Oh, Jaxon," she says, gasping, as I pull a ring from my pocket, holding it before her.

"There's a lot I don't know about you," I tell her. "But the details don't matter. Not when the truth is simple. I love you and want to spend the rest of my life with you. The triplets are the fucking cake—the part we don't deserve, the thing that brought us back together. And I would get you pregnant all over again if it meant I didn't lose you. Tell me I didn't lose you. Tell me you still love me. Tell me you will marry me —because, Harper, I want you to be my wife, so fucking hard."

"Jaxon, yes. A million times, yes," she says, her voice a whisper like a fluttering of joy escaping her lips.

She fucking said yes, just like I prayed she would.

Yeah, I prayed. Because even though I don't need religion to tell me it's a fucking miracle to have this woman, I still thought this was too good to be true.

But it isn't.

I slip the engagement ring on her finger.

"It's beautiful," she says, looking at the simple gold band flanked by three clear diamonds.

"The three diamonds represent our children," I tell her.

"Sons, Jaxon," she says, a grin spreading across her perfect pink lips. "We're having three sons."

I run my hand over my beard, fucking overcome.

"Hell, yeah, we are," I tell her. "We don't mess around."

And then I kiss her, hard. And I would have

fucked here right then too, if a nurse hadn't come in and interrupted us.

"When can she leave?" I ask, knowing it can't come soon enough. I need to get my woman home and make love to her in our bed.

CHAPTER TWENTY-FOUR

HARPER

WHEN THEY DISCHARGE me from the hospital the next morning, I'm grinning. No, scratch that—I'm beaming. I'm absolutely walking on air, because how I ended up here from there still confuses me.

How could I lose my parents but gain a family? Somehow over the space of a few months, Jaxon and I became something that I never believed we could be, not really.

I thought it would be a relationship built from a pressure cooker, but we aren't. He chose me when he didn't have to.

"So, are you ready to get home?" I ask Jaxon as we drive back to the forest, nearing Buck's store to get Jameson.

He turns his head, cocking an eyebrow at me. "Mostly so I can tear those clothes off you and fuck my fiancée."

"I love it when you talk dirty to me, Jaxon."

"Good, because I'm gonna talk that way for the rest of our goddamned life."

We both grin now.

Our life.

When we get to Buck's, Jaxon warns me, "He's gonna want details. But you don't have to say anything you don't wanna."

"That nosy, huh?" I ask, as Jaxon helps me out of the truck.

"This poor fool needs a woman. Bad. Since he doesn't have one, he's become the town gossip."

"You should help the poor boy out," I say, pulling open the door.

"I try," Jaxon says, under his breath. "But he's his own worst enemy when it comes to pussy."

Jameson is curled up at Buck's feet when we walk in, but he must smell Jax, because he jumps up and bounds for his owner.

"Aww, that's so sweet," I coo.

"And who might you be?" Buck asks, stepping around the counter to say hello. He's actually very handsome—blue eyes and light hair. Maybe he just lacks confidence.

"I'm Harper. Jax's fiancée."

"And the mother of my children," Jax says, chest out, beaming.

"Hey, you said this is my story to tell," I tease, jabbing him with my elbow.

"My bad." Jax shrugs.

"Buck," I say. "I'm Jaxon's bride-to-be, and I'm also carrying his three sons." I press my hands to my small belly and relish in Bucks bugged-out eyes.

"Shit, man!" Buck slaps Jaxon on the shoulder. "Had no fucking clue." Then looking at me, he covers his mouth with his fist. "Sorry, ma'am. For the cursing."

"Sweetie," I say to Buck. "I'm marrying Jaxon. I think I can handle a man who swears."

"Thanks for watching Jameson," Jaxon says. "Any deliveries?"

"Nope, but if I get any I'll swing 'em by."

Jaxon and I leave with Jameson, and once we're in the car and headed back up the mountain I ask, "Why does Buck deliver packages to your door?"

"Eh, he's a good guy, likes a chance to talk shit and drink a beer. It can get lonely out here, in the woods."

"Yeah, it is quiet," I say, remembering the empty general store/post office. No one was there—and that was the main store in town.

Besides that, there was just a bar and a sad excuse for a diner.

"You gonna be able to handle this pace of life?" Jaxon asks me. When his hands are on the steering wheel, with his shirtsleeves rolled up, his biceps flex and his tattoos hint at a strength not every man has.

"Jaxon, I grew up with a very quiet life. My world was the home, the church, and the food bank where I volunteered. I don't need much. And, as far as quiet goes...." I smile, and my hands fly to my stomach. "Soon enough, there won't be any quiet in our life. There will be loud and rambunctious, and I have a feeling by the end of the day, once the boys are in bed, all we'll want is to sit in peace and quiet."

"Well, honey, that's where you're wrong," Jaxon says, as he pulls the truck up to the cabin.

"What do you mean?" I ask, my nose crinkled in confusion.

"At the end of the day I'm not gonna want any quiet. I'm gonna want you screaming my name."

JAX

I pull open Harper's car door, pull her into my arms, ready to make love to her like she fucking deserves.

Swinging open my front door, I set her down and grab the bearskin fuck-rug. Then I grab her hand and pull her back outside into the warm April day.

"I'm gonna make you scream my name so loud," I tell her, smacking her ass as I lead her behind the house, to the place she first told me she was pregnant.

There are no deer today, but the creek is rushing peacefully, and I spread out the rug beneath the pine trees.

"I love it here, Jaxon," Harper says contentedly. The buttons on her shirt are pulled tight across her chest. We stopped and got her a bunch of maternity clothes before we left town, but those are all still in the truck.

I sure as hell don't mind. I like the way her tits pull at the seams; it makes me hungry for her.

"I love taking you here, and I love that you're here to stay," I tell her, growling in her ear.

Her eyes are heavy with desire; she loves it when I get territorial, and it's a good thing. I'm determined never to give her a reason to leave.

"Are you going to take me here, now?" she asks, standing before me.

"Do you really have to ask?" I pull my shirt off, and Harper's hands immediately press against my pecs. She nuzzles close to me, her breath hot on my skin, and my cock grows hard pressed against her.

"Oh, baby," she moans, planting kisses up and down my neck lusciously. Her lips are soft and wet, and her tongue slides down my throat as she nears my mouth.

My lips find hers, and I cup her face with my hands, claiming her as mine. She lets out a sigh as I pull her closer, devouring her mouth with my tongue. She tastes so good, sweet and fresh; her scent mixed with the earthy air makes everything about this moment goddamned pure. Goddamned perfect.

"I love you Harper," I breathe into her, and she sighs again, agreeing with my sentiment. I pull her shirt off, the buttons popping as I toss it aside. Her tits are perky and round, those hard gorgeous nipples poking through her lacy bra.

I reach around, unclasp it, and fling it off her. Pressing my mouth against her soft, warm skin, I feel my erection mount, straining against my jeans.

"You feel how hard I am?" I ask her, pushing her hand to feel my cock. "You like how hard you make me?"

"Mmmhhhmmm," she groans, fumbling to get my jeans undone. I help her slide them off, and kick off my shoes and pants, my boxer briefs still on, my massive cock begging to be released.

"What are you gonna do to my cock?' I ask her. "You're the one that got it nice and hard, now you need to take care of it."

"I'm gonna suck it. I'm gonna suck it until you're ready to come."

I smile, so fucking in love with her.

After taking off her pants and panties, she lowers herself to the ground, kneeling before me, and playfully tugs at the waistband of my briefs.

"Jaxon, you're taking such good care of me, and now I'm going to take care of you."

She pulls the waistband down, revealing her favorite fucking thing in the world. My cock is hungry, and it only wants her. She licks her lips seductively.

"That's called a dick tease, Harp."

That gets a throaty laugh from her. "I'm not a tease."

And I have to agree, she's not. Her mouth covers my cock and one hand is on my shaft. The other hand moves south as she touches herself. After rubbing her pussy nice and hard, she brings her hand to my cock, and it's slick with her wetness.

She massages my cock with her own juice, all

the while sucking me off. She bobs up and down, her eyes looking up at me, and I run my hand through her soft hair, not able to look anywhere besides her. Not wanting to.

"Oh, Harper, that feels fucking good," I say, thrusting my cock into her mouth, knowing she likes it when she takes me all the way to the back of her throat.

When I know I'm near release, I pull her off me, wanting to come inside her tight little pussy.

"I want you to sit on me, backwards," I tell her. "It's gonna feel good on your clit, I promise."

I lay on my back, and watch as Harper bites her lip nervously, the way she does when she tries new things. But I also see a mischievous glint of excitement rolling across her face as she lowers herself to her knees.

She leans over, planting a kiss on my lips, and I can't help but reach around her, grab her ass and squeeze. She makes me so fucking hard, and I just want all of her.

Watching her straddle me backwards, I run my hands over her back as she gently lowers her entrance onto my massive rod.

"Ohhh, you're so big," she moans, leaning back, her hair falling across my face as she eases herself around my cock. Her back is arched toward me as she swivels her hips gently.

When I'm inside her, she lifts herself up, grabbing hold of my thighs as she rides me from behind.

I hold her ass cheeks with one hand, my other hand reaching up to her perfect round globes, massaging one as she moves up and down on me.

"Oh, yeah, honey, that's good," I tell her. I'm so turned on by her nice ass and narrow waist, her soft skin and the way she gyrates on top of me.

My cock stretches as it's ready to come, but I want her to come first. I thrust in her, as she swivels faster around my base, and she moans in delight as my groin is covered with her wet pussy. I love it when she pours out her juice for me, when the walls of her pussy explode, releasing all her hotness.

"Oh, Jaxon, fuck me," she says, falling back on my chest again as I thrust harder and deeper into her core. "Fuck me hard."

I love the dirty words coming out of her mouth, her pouty lips moaning in ecstasy.

I can't take it anymore, and I don't want to. I shoot my come in her perfect pussy and she moans, falling forward as the orgasm ripples through both of us.

Her hands grip my thighs tight as she holds on for dear life. When my seed enters her already swollen core, she is undone.

She climbs off me, and kneels close to me, kissing me tenderly.

"Oh, Jaxon ... do we really get this, forever?"

"We do, honey. We do."

CHAPTER TWENTY-FIVE

JAX

My parents arrive a few days after the hospital scare with Harper. She and I are cleaning up breakfast dishes when we hear the RV pull up to the cabin.

"My folks are here," I tell her. I've filled her in on my mom and dad, how they are about as homegrown as you can get, but I know that after the drama with her parents earlier this week nothing about family sounds all that safe right now.

"Do I look all right?" Harper asks. I smirk, never once having heard this woman utter something self-conscious about her appearance. She grew up in a fucked-up house, but one thing her family taught her was that humility was important. Harper never seems caught up in the way she looks.

It reminds me that this really is a big deal. The woman I am engaged to marry, who will give birth to my parents' first three grandsons, is about to meet the people who raised me.

"Harper," I say, tucking a loose strand of hair behind her ear, "you are amazing in too many ways to count. My parents are fools if they don't love you. Fuck, they won't be welcome in my home if they don't recognize how important you are to me. You are my everything."

"Shush," Harper says, pressing her hand over my mouth. She always cuts me off when I compliment her, but it doesn't stop me from letting her know how I goddamned feel.

I pull open the front door, cup of steaming black coffee in my hand. Jameson runs into the driveway, hollering at their ride. Harper sidles up next to me, cream and sugar balancing out her mug. She finds my hand, and I squeeze back, hoping my parents react the way I've been promising her.

Their RV is massive, and it's barely stopped before my mom jumps out, barreling toward us.

"Harper, my darling, look at you!" She's pulling us both into a hug before we can say hello. "I never thought I'd see the day my boy found himself a wife, let alone one as pretty as you. And triplets to boot!"

Harper's blushing within seconds, and I try to suppress a grin. My mom here is going to relieve a hell of a lot of pressure. She's wanted grandkids since I was in high school. Which is weird, but also the motherfucking truth.

"Let the kids breathe, Sandy," my dad calls out, stepping out of their rig.

"Oh, they're fine, Stu." Mom waves Dad off, kissing me on both cheeks. "They've been shacked up in this cabin for a while. It's high time they have some company."

"No one's arguing with that, but you've just met the girl," Dad says, before pulling me into a hug. He then offers my fiancée his hand. "So good to meet you, Harper. And, sweetie, I'm guessing you're a special one if you've decided to spend your life with this fool. Not every woman would be up to the challenge."

"Or want to be," Mom says, then realizing her statement could come off as a little awkward, she waves us into the house. "You know I meant nothing by it, Harper, I'm sure you know the way Jax has been these last ... well, forever. Jax has never found himself wanting to commit. But my guess is, he was just waiting for you."

"I'd like to think that," Harper says, her eyes

wide as she takes in our little family dynamic. Mom speaking her mind, Dad making the peace, and me being the stereotype.

"You got anymore of that coffee?" Mom asks Harper.

"Sure do." Harper and my mom head to the kitchen, where my mom starts asking all sorts of personal and detailed questions about her life, the pregnancy, and her plans for the birth.

I don't want to talk about vaginas with my mother.

"You good, Harper?" I holler. When she nods, I make a beeline out the front door with my dad.

I have a few projects in store for him the next few months, and I need to be sure he intends to stay around.

HARPER

My stomach is officially enormous. I knew it would be big—I mean, triplets—but this is something else. And I still have three months to go.

"These boys are gonna each weigh ten pounds, I swear." I sit in the leatherback chair, trying to catch my breath after climbing down the ladder leading to the loft. "I'm not climbing up there again; it isn't safe," I tell Jaxon, who smiles as he offers me an ice-cold glass of tea.

"Okay, no worries." Jaxon shrugs, his mouth turned into a perfect smirk. Sex appeal drips off him in ways he doesn't even know.

But still. Right now, I have no space for joking. This nesting instinct is real. And the corner of the cabin filled with baby supplies is a growing mountain. I have no idea where it will all go once unpacked. Or where I will even sleep.

"No worries? Jax ... we really need to make a plan with this house. I mean, your mom has been so great with helping us get things for the babies, but last time she took me to town, and we walked around Target—babe, there are a hundred more things we need. And this cabin is...."

"Way too small."

"It is." A sigh escapes my lips. I've been trying not to overthink, not to overanalyze Jaxon's choices ... not to get huffy about the fact he and his dad trudge into the forest all day, every day, chopping wood or whatever they say they are doing. But, as I look around, all I can think is that we need a bigger home.

"Your parent's RV is better equipped to handle the triplets than this cabin is," I say, trying to stay calm. "I've wanted to be positive ... but, Jaxon, this isn't going to work."

"It's just the cabin that isn't working, right, not you and I? Not our life, our plans, right?" Jaxon asks, kneeling before me the same way he did when he proposed. I see the concern written on his face and it warms me to him.

The last few months together have been everything. Jaxon and I are finding a groove. A sometimes awkward, sometimes all-out fight, groove. A groove that gives me rug burn, and a groove that gets him hard when I least expect it.

I often find myself whispering in his ear, urging him to get his parents out of the cabin so we can ... well ... enjoy one another's company.

His parents being here for three months has been an absolute godsend. Sandy and I have sewn a hundred and fifty cloth diapers—which is a lot, but somehow she was game when I suggested the project. I couldn't imagine using disposal diapers and creating that much trash out here in the woods. She and I have spent hours debating baby names as we cut and pin fabric.

And Jaxon and his dad have been in the woods most days; the giant trucks from the mill have come and picked up all the wood he's felled these past months since he moved out here. I'd think they'd be tired of chopping wood day in and day out, but somehow they always come in at the end of the day with sweat-soaked shirts, and filthy dirty.

I don't mind Jaxon taking a shower, I only wish I could join him ... but the baby bump, Jaxon, and I aren't all going to fit in a space that small.

As Jaxon kneels before me, wanting me to confirm that the problem is the cabin and not us, love surges through my heart.

"Of course it's just the cabin." I lean forward, kissing him softly, my lips melting to his instantly. Pulling back, I look into his eyes. "And I'm not trying to be dramatic. Maybe we can make it work. Maybe bring the mattress down here, take out these chairs. Use pack 'n plays instead of cribs." I bite my lip, not knowing how that is realistic.

"Honey, that isn't going to work. Look at this place. It's filled to the max with you and me and the damn dog, and there aren't even any babies here yet."

"I know—but, Jaxon, but where would we go? You don't want to leave the mountain; you've found peace here, your family here. The city only holds bad memories for both of us."

"I know," Jaxon says, his eyebrows knit together as he places his hands on my belly. "I want to stay out here. I can't imagine moving back, working for Dean in town, and putting up with the bullshit of people who don't know how to mind their own business."

"I want to stay out here, too," I tell him truthfully. "I want my boys to grow up here, learn to walk in the green grass and throw pebbles in the rippling creek. I want to make love to you in the shade of the pine trees, and I want to grow old in front of a fire, built from the logs you've hewn."

"Truly, Harper, you'll be okay here? Because I don't want you to sacrifice any more for me. You've given up a hell of a lot already."

"What, like my virginity?" I smile, knowing he likes it when I get haughty. He grins, and a baby does a somersault under his palms. For a moment, the world is still, and our life is complete.

Once the baby settles back down, I run my hands over Jaxon's scruffy, sexy beard, and rub my thumbs over his cheeks. I hold his face in my hands and kiss him softly.

"Jaxon," I say, "our life will be simple, but it will be ours. Not the life my parents tried to carve out for me. I want this life, the life born from the melted snow, that came alive in the gentle spring, that grew in the heat of the summer. I want this life with you, and if that life is built in a six-hundred square foot cabin, so be it."

"This isn't good enough for you, or our sons." Jaxon speaks slowly, his hands still firmly on my tummy. "I want to give you more."

"Baby, don't," I start, shaking my head. I wish I'd never complained, never made him question this life we've chosen.

"No, Harper. It isn't enough." He stands, grabs my hands. "But I will show you what is."

JAX

I wanted to catch her off guard. Wanted to take her breath away. Wanted her to know that, fuck, I've been a bad boy for twenty-eight years, but now I only want to be man. Her man.

And a man takes care of his woman.

Especially a woman as perfect as Harper.

Sure, I proposed, but now I needed her to know I fucking meant what I said. That I'll take care of her and our boys.

"Where are we going?" she asks, as I pull her out the front door.

It's a hot summer day; Harper is in this thin white flowing dress, barefoot, her blonde hair loose around her shoulders.

My parents step out of their RV, where it's been parked for three months.

"Morning, you two. Where you headed?" Dad asks, a gleam in his eye. He knows exactly where we're going.

"Harper, do you need shoes?" my mom calls to my woman.

"I'm good, Sandy. Jaxon's got me."

Holy shit, this woman makes me hard anytime she uses words insinuating that, yeah, she fucking wants me to be her knight in shining armor.

Harper waves good-bye to them as I offer her my hand. She steps into my truck, that curiosity I fell in love with filling her face.

"Where are we going?" she asks, stretching the seat belt over her beautiful belly.

"It's your wedding present."

"We haven't even set a date, Jaxon."

"An early one, then." I wink at her, loving this sweet torture.

"Jaxon, this is totally off-topic, but can I be honest with you for a second?" she says as I put the truck in reverse, backing out of the driveway.

I turn up the mountain before answering.

"Uh, sure," I say. "What's up?"

"I love your parents being here, but, baby, I am so horny lately. Like, I think it's a pregnancy thing. My dreams have been out of this world."

"What kind of dreams?" I turn my head to her, already feeling my cock twitch in my jeans.

"Sex dreams." She buries her head in her hands, and I laugh. Harper can seem so removed from her fucked-up childhood, but then she blushes when she says *sex* and can hardly look at me.

Me, who's seen her naked flesh drenched in sweat, slick with one another as we've made love all night. Me, who has licked her pussy in this car, in the woods, on every surface of the cabin. Me, who has enjoyed her tits as I've come all over them.

She shouldn't be blushing over the word *sex*.

"How sexy are these dreams, Harp?" I ask.

"Very. Like, the most. Like, so sexy that all I want to do is repeat them. But we can't really do that with your parents so close."

"Honey, we've been fucking for a month with their RV right outside the door."

"I know, but ... in these dreams, I'm really loud."

I let out a snort.

"Fuck, I'm glad I'm giving you your present now, because we can practice these sex dreams when we get there."

"We're going somewhere where you swear no one else is? Because I can't have the kind of sex I'm looking to have around anyone else."

"I swear. But, honey, there's no one for miles anywhere on this road."

"Then stop the truck. I can't wait, baby. I need you now."

"Are you for real?" I ask, shaking my head. I'm about to give this woman a surprise, and all she wants is an orgasm.

"Jaxon, can you stop? Please?" She reaches under her dress and unclasps her bra, maneuvering herself out of it. She pulls it out of her dress and tosses it on the truck bench. "I'm about to lose my mind. I need you. Like, ten minutes ago.

"Good lord, Harper." She is a crazed, horny, pregnant woman, and—surprise be damned—I can't help but love her enthusiasm.

I park off the side of the road, and she nearly jumps out of the truck.

"Come on," she hollers. "Not car sex, I need you to take me against a tree."

My eyes almost jump out of my head, but this woman isn't joking.

"You're unbelievable," I tell her, following as she darts into the woods. Pine needles cover the forest floor—thankfully, as Harper is barefoot. She doesn't seem to mind; her mind is singularly focused. "You sure you're not scared of a bear?"

"Are there bears here?" she asks, whipping her head back toward me.

"No, calm down." I don't tell her that, hell yeah, there are bears. We're in the fucking forest.

She stops in the middle of the path, a fallen log covered in velvety green moss cutting us off from traipsing deeper.

"Here," she says, her voice filled with desire. "I want you here." She reaches down to the hem of her dress, lifting it over her head. Her pussy is bare—I have no fucking clue where her panties went—and her tits are full, round globes, waiting to be sucked.

I pull my tee shirt over my head and unbuckle my belt, unzip my pants, take everything off.

We stand naked, in the woods. The timber around us is strong, reaching to the sky, and our toes sink into the earth, and I feel grounded like I never have before.

Harper is before me and all I want to do taste her skin and lick her curves, and press my growing wood into her wet opening.

"Your cock is so hard," she whimpers, her hands running over her breasts, her nipples hard and tight as she thumbs them softly, licking her lips as she looks me over.

"And you like it hard, don't you, Harper?"

"I like it so hard," she says, pulling her hair back, exposing more of her beautiful belly.

Her skin is stretched over the roundness of our boys, and she is a fucking miracle, standing there like a forest goddess or a nymph. All that's missing are her goddamned wings. This woman isn't made for the earth. She's an angel, and she's mine.

I pull her to me, her soft skin crushing against the strength of my body. My muscles have been worked the past few months like they've never been before. My stomach is chiseled, and my biceps flex as I wrap my arms around her.

"Baby," she breathes into my chest, kissing my pecs, running her hands across the expanse of my back. "I'm so wet for you."

My hand reaches between her legs, where her entrance is dripping with desire, and I press my finger into her, thumbing her clit slowly, methodically, knowing my woman likes to build up to her release.

"You like it when I touch?" I ask her.

"I like it when you fuck me," she says, pushing me toward the fallen log.

I stretch out atop the mossy log, and my cock stands at attention before her.

"Your cock is so good to me," Harper moans, as she walks to where I'm laying out for her, taking my jeans and balling them up, before tucking them beneath me as a pillow.

"Show me how good it is," I tell her, wrapping a hand around her thigh as she climbs atop me.

She straddles my thighs, and leans down to press her mouth to my throbbing cock. My whole member tightens as she takes so much of me between her lips. She tightens her mouth around me, bobbing up and down, as my veiny cock hardens even more. Her hands press between her legs, and she rubs her pussy juice over my shaft, running her hand up and down as she sucks me off.

"Oh, yeah, honey." I groan as she rolls my balls in her hand, massaging them tenderly, but also explosively. I'm gonna come in her mouth if she keeps going at this pace.

She pulls my cock out, licking my tip in fast circles that cause pre-come to release, and she licks that, too, as if my cock is a fucking popsicle.

"You taste so good," she says, moving forward so she can press my hard rod into her pussy. Sitting down on me, she whimpers as a smile slowly spreads across her face.

"That how loud things got in your sex dream?" I ask, teasingly.

"Not even close, Jaxon." She pants out the words, a deep guttural moan growing from within her. She slaps my chest, her belly between us, but not hindering our love making at all.

I thrust up, wanting to rock her deep and hard, cause her to let go like a wild animal.

It works; her moaning turns to yelps as she grinds against my massive cock. She buries me inside her, her feet balancing on the forest floor as she straddles me like a motherfucking bull rider.

Her tits bounce as she rides me, swiveling her hips as she edges closer to pleasure. My chest is covered in sweat as I thrust harder into her perfect pussy, her juice pouring over my thighs—and I fucking love it when that happens, when she gushes her desire all over my skin.

I slap her ass, so turned on by being in the wild with her, my woman, who likes it hard and rough, who's begging me to grind deeper into her core.

She loves fucking me. It's as if her pussy and my cock were made for one another. Her tight pussy lips wrap so good around my rod, and I want to get her off even more. I press my fingers at her opening, rubbing in circles as she rotates above me.

Her back arches as she gasps in desire, her wailing giving way to full-on screams of ecstasy.

Now *this* is a motherfucking sex dream.

I thrust again, and again, until my come shoots from my throbbing cock into her core. She stills as the wave of the orgasm unleashes itself through her. She presses her hands to my chest, gripping me as it flows through her.

"Oh. My. God. Jaxon." She hollers my name as she's overcome.

I can't help but think this woman is gonna be a force to be reckoned with when she goes into labor.

She can't lay down on top of me, not with her pregnant belly, so instead she climbs off me and I sit up. Then she straddles the tree again, this time with her back pressed against my chest. I wrap my arms around her gorgeous stomach, our fresh, sexed smell mixing with the dirt and the moss, the pine trees and the great outdoors.

Later, we dress, make our way back to the truck, a satisfied smile written on her face and a cocky grin surely on mine. I start the truck and her hand finds mine. She laces her fingers through mine as I turn back to the road.

She has no fucking clue what I've done for her.

We drive up the hill, only a short mile more, and turn off onto a still unpaved road. The pavement will happen later. For now, my crew and I have only focused on the structure.

When we turn onto the road, the tires grinding over the long, tree-covered dirt road, Harper looks at me again, almost asking a question. Then she stops before any words leave her lips.

I had a sign made. It reads *Doe Cabin* and, as we pass it, Harper can't muster any more restraint.

"Whose house are we going to?" she asks.

I don't answer; I wait until we've rounded the corner, and the home is in plain view.

"Our house."

"Jaxon," she says, her voice catching on her emotion. "When? How? Really?"

She grabs my hand, taking in the beautiful two-story log cabin, with the wrap-around porch, the stone chimney, the double-front doors that beckon for us to enter.

I smile slyly and get out of the truck, stepping around quickly to her door to help her out. Her eyes are filled with glistening tears, the same bewildered look she had the first night I met her, when she came to my front door in the middle of a snowstorm. When her pale blue eyes met mine, I had no chance of looking anywhere else, ever again.

Harper had me the moment we met.

"I built this home for you, Harper. For our family."

"All those logs from the yard ... those are here? Built into this house?"

"Every last one. But a lot more, too. Dean wanted to expand our business into custom homes, and our place is the first one we built. My dad did all the carpentry work."

"In three months? You all did this in three months, for me?"

"Well, to be fair, some days we'd have a crew of thirty men up here." I take her hand and we cross the stone walkway toward the porch. Trees surround us in every direction and mountain peaks rise above them.

"So it wasn't just the trucks from the wood mill cutting up the mountain everyday?"

I shake my head, unlocking the front door. "Wanna see inside?"

Harper stops, not taking a step in.

"This feels momentous," she says, her eyes filled with love and light. "It's like the first step into our new life."

"Then, honey, let me carry you over the threshold of our forever."

EPILOGUE

FIVE MONTHS LATER...

HARPER

THE CABIN IS WARM, a glowing fire keeping us warm on this February night. The forest green upholstered rocker was a baby gift from Dean, and I appreciate that his current girlfriend helped him pick it out as it matches the lodge-esque interior of my hand-built home.

I cradle Cedar as I nurse him to sleep, marveling at his little nose and his tiny mouth nestled against my skin, suckling as he falls into slumber.

Cedar is my smallest babe, but not by much. The triplets, born six weeks early, weren't ten pounds a piece as I'd feared, but his brothers were each a pound and a half heavier–seven!–than little Cedar.

"Alder and Spruce are out," Jaxon says from upstairs, taking the steps two at a time as he comes into the great room.

"Shhh," I say, running my hand over Cedar's head. "You'll wake him."

"I got this, honey," he says, coming over and taking Cedar from my arms. Milk drool escapes his heart-shaped lips, and Jaxon expertly positions him in his arms.

I follow Jaxon upstairs to where the boys sleep in their cradles in our master bedroom.

Jaxon sets Cedar in his, making sure he is tightly swaddled.

"I can't believe they're all sleeping at the same time," I say, my eyes fighting to stay open.

The past four months have been every bit as hard as I feared, but I constantly look at the framed print Jaxon hung in our room.

Last year at this time, when I was left a week before my wedding, lost in a snowstorm, looking for a savior, *Keep Calm and Carry On* was the motto I claimed for myself. It has never been more timely—because, oh my heart, triplets are a lot of work.

"I think we all need to try to sleep at the same time," Jaxon says, wrapping his arms around my much-flatter-but-not-nearly-the-same stomach.

"Really, Jaxon, you wanna sleep right now?" I ask, suddenly awake. "Because alone time with my sexy lumberjack is not something I have that often."

"In that case, I'll show you some wood."

We both start to laugh at his cheesy line, the line that has actually worked on me more times than I'd like to admit.

But then immediately we clap our hands over one another's mouths.

Sex may be on the table, but keeping the babies asleep is most important.

Life is funny like that. Things change, priorities shift. I have an engagement ring on my finger but I'm not racing to get married. Right now I have more than enough.

Right now, I have all I need.

-THE END-

I hope you have loved
Jaxon and Harper's
love story!
Ready for more in this ovary-exploding world?!
There are four more stories set on this fertile
mountain!

The Mountain Man's Babies:

<u>TIMBER</u>

<u>BUCKED</u>

<u>WILDER</u>

<u>HONORED</u>

<u>CHERISHED</u>

<u>BUILT</u>

<u>CHISELED</u>

<u>HOMEWARD</u>

<u>RAISED</u>

PREVIEW

BUCKED: The Mountain Man's Babie

I want two things in life: a woman and a child. When I walk into the diner and see Rosie, I think my motherf*cking dreams have come true.

We share one stolen afternoon, but then she's gone.

Eight months later she shows up at my cabin.

Her belly swollen, her breasts full, and with the face of an angel.

Still, she wants to keep on running.

No way in hell am I letting her go.

It's not just Rosie that needs my protection—our babies do too.

Darling You,

BUCKED is a stand alone story that is packed

with true love and a man who knows what he wants: his woman. He fights for her like a real mountain man knows how to do! I hope you love it to pieces—I had so much fun working on it with you in mind! Also, if you loved TIMBER, Jax and Harper (and their babies!) are in Buck and Rosie's story too!

xo, frankie

Download here: BUCKED: The Mountain Man's Babies

ABOUT THE AUTHOR

Frankie Love writes filthy-sweet stories about bad boys and mountain men.

As a thirty-something mom who is ridiculously in love with her own bearded hottie, she believes in love-at-first-sight and happily-ever-afters.

She also believes in the power of a quickie.

Find Frankie here:

www.frankielove.net